SPEAKER OF WORDS

E. G. STONE

INDIEOWL PRESS

INDIEOWL
PRESS

4700 Millenia Blvd
Ste 175 #90776
Orlando, FL 32839

info@indieowlpress.com
IndieOwlPress.com

SPEAKER OF WORDS

Cover Design & Interior Layout by NightOwlFreelance.com
Cover art © Spy Tech Illustrations

Paperback ISBN-13: 978-1-949193-72-5
Softcover ISBN-13: 978-1-949193-61-9
Hardcover ISBN-13: 978-1-949193-73-2

This book is dedicated to everyone who helped me chase my dream of being a writer, and who listened to the words never said.

SPEAKER OF WORDS

"The chief merit of language is clearness,
and we know that nothing distracts as much
from this as do unfamiliar terms."
—Galen

The empty cargo-hold of the speeder had three words scrawled on the side in bright red letters: *Nehrun tai hanen.* The spectacle—no doubt that it was meant to be—was in the middle of the largest and busiest speeder pass in Kyper City. Thank the Republic it was early enough that the curious crowds weren't overwhelming the security force.

A security speeder approached and drew to a stop, its lift engines cutting as it lowered gently to the ground. The hatch opened and the officers of the force straightened, eyes flashing, they tugged at their uniforms for a better fit. A man climbed out, wearing black trousers and military-cut jacket under an overcoat of camel-coloured synthetics. A silver insignia was inscribed on his lapel: a circle superimposed on the symbol of infinity. He stood with the confidence of someone with a lifetime of experience in the security forces, and his attire confirmed that. He was lean, every inch of him honed with hours of rigorous training and minimal sleep, not a slate-grey hair out of place. Only his eyes, dark deep green and surrounded by fine lines, showed any emotion.

That morning, the emotion was weariness.

"Inspector Dawes," one of the security men approached the newcomer and saluted, straightening his posture. Dawes nodded and returned the salute. "Greetings, Citizen! Officer Kasey, sir, ready to assist."

"What's the story, Kasey?" Dawes asked, frowning as he took in the local force Officer.

"The cargo speeder was carrying medical supplies. Raw stuff, to make the finer pharmaceuticals, bandages, food rations, the works. It was raided at three this morning. There wasn't time for the crew to pull any weapons, though the supervisor managed to raise an alarm. By the time security forces arrived, it was like this. Empty with the words graffitied on the side." Kasey walked around the side of the speeder, Dawes following, and the words came into stark view. Bright as freshly spilled blood — not even dulled by the forensic crews' attempt to remove them from the side of the speeder.

"What does it mean?" Dawes asked, more to himself than anything. Kasey shook his head and shrugged, one hand on his holstered bully stick.

"We don't know," Kasey said. "This is the third instance of a raid with those words. Then there are the others."

"Others"? The reality of the situation was beginning to dawn on Dawes. His superiors had shuffled the case to him, sending him in from Kyper Central, telling him to deal with the situation or there would be repercussions. He figured it was a simple bash-and-dash that some of the local outcasts had caused. He hated bash-and-dashes. It was an insult that there were violent crimes at all, but defacement of Republic property was particularly grating. Occasionally, there was the one-off spot of vandalism or bash-and-dashes. Others, though, meant something more. Meant that the attackers were dissidents. Enemies of the Republic. And now, here he was, dealing with those fools on the local security force, just being told that this was the latest in a series. Dawes shoved his hands into his pockets and tightened them into fists.

Kasey nodded, "The local force has inspected four spots of vandalism with words in some unknown language. The paint is the same stuff as what's on this speeder. Impossible to remove. We can paint over it, but it takes three or four coats. Nasty compound."

"What about the other raids?" Dawes asked. He wanted to do as had been done to him: shunt this work on someone else. But the local forces had asked for help from Kyper Central. They were security, the forces argued. Meant to protect the people and enforce rules, not deal with raids against Republic property. That was what Kyper Central was for—protecting the interest of the Republic. Dawes supposed he should have been glad that the Republic Military Intelligence wasn't involved. That would get messy.

"Oh," Kasey frowned, his youth and Placement showing through his inexperience. "Three others, all with 'nehrun tai hanen' at the scene. Two against business-class vessels, one other against a medical shipment. There is no forensic evidence at the scene, apart from the paint, and none of the speeder crews can remember anything."

"Why not?" Dawes asked. If they witnessed the attack, they should remember. It was all he had, and he needed it to be there. He wanted an easy day's work, not this. Not this close to his fifty-years of service celebration.

"Because they were doped with Dreamscape." Kasey rubbed the back of his neck nervously. Dawes cursed and slammed his fist into the side of the empty speeder. His fist rang with the energy, and the metal of the speeder vibrated. More than defacement of Republic property, he hated drug users. They were failures, incompetent, and unintelligent failures, incapable of being satisfied with all that the Republic provided. Ungrateful, more than outcasts, they were weak. And all too pervasive.

"How bad?" Dawes asked, all of his hopes for the day drowned in mud. Anytime Dreamscape got involved, things were bad.

"Seven in rehabilitation. Others out on sick leave. We haven't had a problem with Dreamscape until these raids. Things were clean out this way," Kasey's words sounded almost like a whine. Dawes lost the last control over his temper and rounded on the officer.

"Just because you incompetent fools weren't aware of a problem doesn't mean that it wasn't there. Do you have any idea how *addictive* Dreamscape is? What it does to you?" Dawes drew in close to Kasey, his lips drawn in a snarl.

Kasey swallowed and nodded, skin flushed.

Disgusted, Dawes stepped away from the security officer and took three deep breaths to calm himself. He knew what he would be told if it were discovered that he had lost his temper once again. It would be worse if he hit the idiot. For good measure, Dawes took another three breaths.

He had to interact with Kasey, but only as long as this job demanded. Do the work, get back to the offices, and no more interaction with the security forces. Not unless Kasey put in an official request. By the Republic, if Dawes had to deal with any more of this incompetence, he would hit something. And it wouldn't be a metal speeder, this time.

"I want every scrap of information that you have on these raids and the vandalism copied to a data crystal within the hour. You are going to put it into my hands, and then I am going to officially take over the investigation. Anything that Kyper Central wants, you do it, am I clear?" Dawes hissed, keeping his eyes fixed on Kasey's face.

"Absolutely," Kasey said. "You'll have everything you need."

Dawes curled his lip and turned away, going back to his speeder and sitting in the seat. "Take me to Kyper Central," Dawes murmured. The speeder whirred to life and did as it was told, the lift engines pulling air through the intake and using the heat differential to power the drive. It rose into the air and darted off, inertial dampeners flicking on a moment after motion began. Dawes was oblivious to all of this and stared blankly at the elaborate architecture of Kyper City, the buildings rising a mile into the air, connected by sky bridges and speeder pathways were a blur. He was too busy cursing his superiors and the people who had hindered the success of the raid.

He would do his job, Dawes knew. The problem wasn't whether he would do his job, it was that he would do it to perfection. There was no task Dawes could be given that he would do half-heartedly. He was tired of being handed cases others considered nearly impossible because his superiors knew he wouldn't rest until it was solved, or he was dead. He had been working for K.C. for almost fifty years and, at seventy-two, he was months away from getting his Official Decommissioning: a final commendation plus stipend that the Republic granted all service members until their death. As young as he was, it was likely to be another forty years before he died. There was no doubt in Dawes' mind that he deserved generous recompense, especially given situations like this one.

People in the Republic were so ignorant. So protected in their little communities. They didn't interact with those outside their Placement unless it was necessary. And they didn't know about the things Dawes had seen over the years that would threaten their sense of security and blissful ignorance. For the disillusionment alone, Dawes was pretty sure he deserved more than a generous recompense.

The speeder pulled into the bay and Dawes disembarked, schooling his expression as he walked into the doors.

The well-cut suits seemed to edge around him as he walked past, no one stopping to make eye contact, not even the braver of the Politicos, those envoys to the Konsulars. A few pointedly looked at the floor, ignoring the fact that their status within the Republic was much greater than his. Dawes thought he knew the reason for this, that it might have something to do with the fact that he couldn't control his anger. It was another reason why he got stuck with the nastiest jobs his superiors could throw at him. Mainly taking care of the dissidents. And dealing with people who were far out of his purview.

Dawes tensed his jaw as he leaned forwards and allowed the retinal scanner to search his eye. The door to his office slid open and he waited until the metal had sealed again before releasing a breath. He paused for three beats, long enough to see the familiar metal room, the desk, the sparse decorations. A moment later, he was whirling around, slamming his already-bruised fist into the wall. The metal, a new compound that every government building in the Republic was coated with, didn't even wobble. It was meant to withstand explosions. One attack from an angry man wouldn't even leave a mark.

Dawes pulled his hand away, feeling the broken bones and cursing. He couched his arm against his body and walked over to a panel in the wall. "Password: Mine," he breathed. The wall clicked and opened, revealing four vials. He took one and injected it into his injured arm, swallowing as the healing nanites contained within started to work. Illegal, he knew. But they were only good for one healing before the building's background radiation killed them off. The evidence would be gone soon. One perk of the job: knowing they existed. Another perk: no one bothered to find out that he had acquired some.

He flexed and the bones snapped back into place. He screamed. Thankfully, the metal of the walls was soundproof as well. Another benefit of working for K.C. was the Privacy Monitors didn't have authority to monitor personal offices. Dawes settled into the chair at his desk and wished that he hadn't given up drinking. He had wanted to be sober for his Decommissioning, so that he could fully enjoy the feeling of absolute release when he was finally free of K.C. That day was farther off than before, and the chemical craving was rearing its head.

"Visitor for Inspector Maddox Dawes," a pleasant female voice intoned, her words whispery and calming. Dawes wished the computer had an adjustable setting, but it was unchangeable. He would have preferred something that didn't make him feel quite so shameful.

He shook that thought away. "Enter," he said, his voice rough from the pain of the nanites still coursing through his hand. He could feel the healing working and kept his hand below his desk, out of sight, in case whoever walked through that door actually cared. When Officer Kasey entered, looking grim and angry, it was plain that he wouldn't care.

Kasey stepped forwards and put a single black data crystal on the glass surface of Dawes' desk. "Greetings, Citizen. This is all the information we have on the raids and the graffiti. The medical records of the people dosed with Dreamscape. Vids and stills of the sites. Specs on the speeders. Everything."

"What about other instances of Dreamscape in the area?" Dawes asked, ignoring the official greeting. He was the superior Placement. He didn't need to respond. Kasey paled, his skin taking on a grey tinge, and shook his head. "Get that to me by tomorrow evening."

"Of course, Inspector," Kasey said. He straightened to attention and jerked his head in a traditional security forces bow. Dawes watched him for a moment and Kasey took that as his cue to leave.

"Wait," Dawes said, a small part of him enjoyed watching the youngling squirm. After all, it was part of the job, part of earning your way up the ladder. "Have you handed off any information of the graffiti to an Interface"?

"Interface?" Kasey asked. Dawes silently cursed himself. Of course, the district security forces wouldn't have access to everything that Kyper Central did. Interfaces were almost essential in Central offices. They worked with the computers, analysing the massive amounts of data that the Republic produced, instead of reading it raw.

"Interfaces," Dawes clarified, hoping that Kasey just didn't understand the lingo. "Computer speakers. Or even the Caretakers to the Interfaces. Anything?"

"Our Interface access hasn't been updated for nearly a decade. We only have basic functioning and security data access." Kasey shook his head, this time stepping backwards in an obvious retreat. He was nearly at the door and Dawes wasn't in the mood to stop him. "We don't have enough need for a computer speaker or Caretaker or whatever you want to call it. We use the basic computer systems to compile data and look for patterns. We have to read the raw data. Sometimes we even do it by hand."

Dawes shuddered at the inefficiency. He closed his eyes for an instant to ruminate in the fact that humans were just not capable of great pattern-thought. Kasey took that instant to escape. When Dawes opened his eyes again, Kasey was gone, the black crystal the only evidence that he had been there at all. Fine.

Dawes took the crystal with his almost-healed hand and slid it into the data port, whispering, "Open all files, wall spread." The computer did as it was told. Files on the crystal opened and holographic images spread throughout the room. This was one of the reasons why he didn't mind not having a window in the office. It was easier to see the important things. The computer automatically organised the files in Dawes' preferred manner, putting like things with each other. The raids against speeders—four in total—went by the wall behind Dawes' desk. The two business-class vessels were positioned together, the medical-class vessels the same. Manifests were opened, and beside each, a paused vid and collection of stills. The other instances of pure vandalism were put on the left wall when facing the door. Three of those, red words written out in a precise hand: *Nehrun tai hanen.*

It must mean something.

"Computer, send the files related to the graffiti to an Interface. Maybe two, if their current workload permits. Get them working on it, see if anything comes up," Dawes said. The computer gave a ping when the job was done, and Dawes nodded. He lifted his hands and spread his fingers, expanding the data projected on the walls to cover every inch of space. Then Dawes stood and stepped closer, looking over every detail. Missing nothing.

What he discovered was this: there was nothing spectacular about any of the speeders or spots chosen for vandalism. Apart from the fact that two speeders were business-class and two were medical-class, they were different. Different models, different speed specs and lift capabilities, even different defence grids. The supplies taken from the medical-class ships were different, too. Some contained medicine, some contained only the supplies for making medicine as well as other items like thermo blankets and bandages. The business-class speeders were only missing the files that were carried on them, the data mostly harmless. The only similarities were the words.

It was the same story with the sites of vandalism. They were in different parts of the district, some in the centre, some near the border, some on buildings, some on sky bridges. Again, the only similarities were the words.

Always those three words. *Nehrun tai hanen.* It must mean something significant. No senseless acts of vandalism would require the repetition of the words. That meant that these vandals were definitely dissidents. And dissidents always had a message to convey. Maybe this was their signature. Maybe it was a call to arms. Maybe it was a warning to the Republic. If that were the case, then why shroud the message with secrecy?

Once the nanites in Dawes' hand were dead—which took three hours, by his clock—he swiped his hand through the air in a furious motion, turning off the projected images and locking the file in a flash. He approached the door to his office and snarled in frustration when it didn't open the second he wanted. When it finally did open, he stalked through and went to the speeder bay, calling his speeder up and demanding that he be taken home. He really needed that drink.

Halfway through the ride, as Dawes was passing the enormous holoscreens that played clips of the Republic leaders and extolled their successes, something happened. Something that made this insignificant investigation impossibly important.

The holoscreens blacked out.

A second later, three words appeared in bright, murderous red: *Nehrun tai hanen.*

Dawes' speeder immediately stopped moving, working under a directive sent out from Republic Transport Command that controlled all speeders in case of an emergency. It was slightly disconcerting, seeing the speeders hanging against the near-darkness of the twilight sky, silhouetted and unmoving against the backdrop of the lights from the city. The holoscreens were still black, still displaying those words, though Dawes knew that the techs in charge of them would be using their best Interfaces to try and thwart the attack.

Minutes passed. Not a single speeder moved, as far as Dawes could see. Republic Transport Command must have the entire city on lock-down. The screens flickered. He raised his eyebrows expectantly. Nothing changed, those words still illuminating the now-dark sky. Dawes would have hoped that the Head of State would have come on the Aircom system, proclaiming that everything was alright and there was no reason for alarm, that there was just a glitch in the system and people needn't worry. Dawes would know better, but the words would still be comforting. To hear that there were still people out there instead of just him, alone, suspended in his speeder.

After another fifteen minutes or so, there was enough worry in Dawes to rise up to the surface. He tried taking manual control of the speeder, giving his credentials and passcodes, demanding that the computer relinquish control.

"Action not possible at this time," the female voice of the computer intoned. Dawes smashed the console with the base of his fist, hoping that would knock some sense into the stupid machine. It did not.

The screens displaying the words *Nehrun tai hanen* flickered again, then went completely dark and finally lit again, once more displaying vids of politicians and advertisements for Republic-sponsored vacations or recruitment offers. Not a single mention of what had happened. The Aircom system remained quiet inside the speeder, even as the machine began moving again, following Dawes' original course.

"Call Daleni Itar, Head of K.C.," Dawes demanded. He didn't really have the authority to contact Daleni Itar directly, but he didn't care. She knew him. And the circumstances were dire enough to warrant the breach in protocol.

The computer complied, bringing up an image of the Head of Kyper Central's office. A large-boned woman ten years younger than Dawes and with skin the colour of ebony depicting her heritage as one of the desert-people of Jushpe, was moving her hands over the surface of her desk with speed, searching her own computer Interface for something.

"Greeting, Citizen," she said in a low voice, looking up at him.

"Citizen," he responded, voice grim.

"Maddox, what is going on out there? All I know is that one minute everything is running as normal and then the computers freeze up. That damn message, 'action not possible at this time' is all I could get the idiotic thing to say. I'm not an Interface or CB to get in and actually force the stupid thing to do what I want."

"Someone hijacked the main screens. Same piece of lingo that I found on my bash-and-dash this morning," Dawes said. "Nehrun tai hanen. I don't even know if I'm saying that right. But it was on the screens for a good twenty minutes before the Republic managed to get control back. The Aircom system was completely silent. Nothing from the Head of State or anyone. All speeders went dark, too, just sitting there."

"That's probably an emergency protocol by Republic Command, in case some dissident breaks through," Daleni Itar said. She let out a hiss through her teeth, eyes flashing. "I thought we had gotten rid of those damn rebels after the last revolt. Opinion polls have been up seventy percent over the last two years. People are *happy*."

"This could be a new group. Dreamscape use is on the rise, and you know that always makes the addicts a bit antsy. Just a minute, I have to transfer," Dawes said. His speeder pulled into the personal bay of his flat and he flicked his wrist, transferring the call to his display walls. Dawes walked through the door from the bay into his flat, noting with pleasure the simple lines of his white walls and dark flooring. Everything has a purpose and is in its place. Order. Simplicity. Perfection. Just as the Republic worked.

"You said that you had something similar? A bash-and-dash?" Daleni Itar asked as soon as Dawes was in sight again.

He nodded and took off his overcoat, hanging it on its designated hook in the closet. "Yeah, got handed down to me this morning by the head of the Security Forces. Told me to take care of it. Someone robbed a medi-speeder this morning, got away with everything before the crew's call for help could be answered. Crew was dosed with Dreamscape, doesn't remember who attacked. Same words were written on the side of the speeder."

"Did you get an Interface to look into it"? Dawes unbuttoned the first clip on his uniform jacket and got out a glass and a bottle of dark amber, thank-the-Republic liquor. He took a sip and sighed, letting out a breath that he felt like he had been holding forever.

"Of course, I did," he said. "I've been doing this job for nearly fifty years. I'm going to be Decommissioned in a month."

"That's not going to happen, Maddox," Daleni Itar said. She shuffled her fingers on her interface again and frowned.

"What?" Dawes said, almost afraid to ask. His whole day had gone from bad to worse and now his Decommissioning was being dashed to the side. He loved the Republic, just as he had been raised, but sometimes it was almost too much. He didn't say anything else, though, because he knew the answer would be along the lines of 'we work on the darker aspects of things so that the citizens of the Republic can have safe, happy lives.' He just took another sip of the liquor.

"I looked at the request that you filed with the Interfaces. Nothing," she answered.

Dawes drew his brows together and was about to ask a question when she continued.

"I mean they state that they cannot decipher the meaning of *Nehrun tai hanen* and that we should focus our investigation elsewhere. Look for other patterns in the modes of attack on the transports. Transports? I thought that yours was a one-off."

"No," Dawes finished off his drink. "It's not."

"You know that I'm going to have the Head of State breathing down my neck in a matter of minutes, don't you? Wanting to know what it all means." Daleni's tone was darkening, trending towards a growl. Dawes could do nothing and just shrugged.

"I don't know anything about language. I mean, I'm just assuming it's part of a language because if it's being written on the side of speeders, then it has to mean something, right? This is more than some dissident signature marking territory," Dawes said. "But if it's not a language, I don't know what it is."

"No, you're probably right. It must be a message. Maddox—Great, just great. I'm going to have to let you go, Maddox. You had better keep working on this. You're the only thing standing between me and the Rabesh Colony right now." Daleni Itar fixed her gaze on Dawes' and curled her lip in anger. "I *do not* want to go to a work colony. Am I clear? Goodbye, Citizen."

The call ended.

Dawes walked over to his window and looked out over the sky city of Kyper, noting that the usual amount of speeder traffic had dissipated, probably because people were afraid after the attack earlier.

14

He closed his eyes and rubbed the bridge of his nose. "Perfectly clear," Dawes said, feeling very much like a headache was coming on. "Absolutely, perfectly, frustratingly clear."

2

Morning did not find Dawes any happier than he had been the night before. The Caretakers had repeated the message from the Interfaces that it would be prudent to look elsewhere for answers. Apparently, *Nehrun tai hanen* meant nothing. There was no record of anyone talking like that anywhere in the Republic, let alone Kyper, and the historical records had no information, either. As far as the Interfaces could tell, it was a useless ploy to make more of the situation than it was. Also, the Interfaces had somehow been diverted during the attack and it still hadn't been determined how that happened.

Dawes grumbled to himself the whole way to K.C. He should be retiring. Only a few months of smaller jobs, enough to prove he was still working but indicating—quite clearly, thank you—that he was on his way out. Instead, someone handed him a bash-and-dash connected to what *could* turn out to be one of the largest attacks by the dissidents since the open revolt. And everyone knew how *that* had ended.

"Dawes to Interface Offices. Dawes to Interface Offices," the pleasant female voice said as he walked in.

"Message received," Dawes snarled. "On my way." Great, now he had to go deal with the Interfaces. He threw his overcoat at his chair and stalked out of the room. The few people he passed in the hallway glanced at him nervously. He wasn't surprised. Most people working for K.C. were thrilled to have been Placed there. Dawes was not. The disparity between him and the others made things tense. At least he wasn't on Rabesh or Crepuscule or something. The Carthinian Islands might be nice, though. A good place to settle after Decommissioning.

Pleasant thoughts of the islands were disrupted as Dawes walked into the Interface Offices. He shuddered once then carefully put his emotions under control, should the Interfaces take note and add it to his file. Those machines saw everything.

"Greetings, Citizen. Ah, Inspector Dawes," a snivelling voice said. Dawes turned to face the man in charge of Interface Operations and pushed away the desire to shudder again.

"Greetings, Citizen," Dawes returned gruffly, hunching his shoulders slightly.

The man was more like a creature than anything, with a twisted spine and shuffling gait, wide eyes that hardly ever saw daylight, and a slight hesitation to his voice as though he were unaccustomed to speaking at all. Given the surroundings, Dawes wouldn't have been surprised if that were true. Interface Offices was nothing more than a huge sub-basement to K.C., the only place the temperature was low enough to keep the Interfaces. As a result, it was dark, cold, and the air smelled like a hospital: sterile and full of chemicals. Along each wall were alcoves where the Interfaces sat, their bodies held still by the numerous tubes and lines running from them. A tube to keep the body alive, with liquid nutrients running through it; a line to connect the computer to the Interface's brain and to the collective. The most disturbing part was that the computer was partly interfaced into the motor cortex. The result was that Interfaces twitched as they encountered new data, like corpses that had not quite tasted death.

It was an honour, supposedly, to be considered compatible with the Interface system. You had to be of above-average intelligence and of the right health. Interfaces, like others, were Placed from childhood and, while it was possible to decline, most people didn't. Who would? Having access to all the knowledge in the Republic? Sure, there were privacy monitors, but that was only for getting the information out of the Interfaces and into the public. If you were directly tied to a computer, though, there was no privacy. You could know everything. And the enhanced brain-power the computer afforded as it tapped into the neurons meant that you could do almost anything.

Except, apparently, decipher three unknown words.

"Yes," Dawes said, forgetting the man's name. The caretaker probably knew that fact, but he just smiled wider, giving him a desperate sort of look. "Is there a reason why you called me here"?

"Only to clarify the lack of response to your request regarding the words. I understand that your case is to be given top priority." He chuckled, amused for some unknown reason. Dawes said nothing. "The Interfaces can do nothing."

"So I've been told," Dawes replied drily. "Why not"?

"Because they have no records of such things. Any language relating to these words does not exist. And without more information, more samples to work from, there is nothing my Interfaces can do. We will continue to analyse the other information regarding the speeders that were hit, the paint compound, even the cyberattack of last night, but the words we can do nothing about."

"How can you have no record of such a thing?" Dawes demanded. He swept his arm out to the Interfaces in their alcoves. "They have access to all current and historical data—including recorded conversation—

in the Republic. How can they *not* be aware?"

"There is no record. That means that whoever did this is careful. You are going to have to look elsewhere for answers, Inspector." The caretaker sniffed. Dawes ground his teeth to keep from hitting the little man.

"And where would you suggest I go to do *that*? You have given me next to no information on the crimes, and there has been no mention of the Dreamscape that the people were dosed with. If this has been given such high priority, then where is my information?" Dawes demanded.

He had nothing if he didn't get information from the Interfaces. The words had been his best lead and, now, he was told there was no record. How was that even possible? The Republic recorded everything. There were very few places that a person wasn't recorded. The reason for that was so that people like Dawes could call on the Interfaces and find the perpetrators of crimes. The people accepted the recordings in place of safety. And there was the added protection of the privacy monitors, so there were next to no issues with that system. The fact that the words hadn't been recorded was impossible. And extremely frustrating.

"There is one person who may be able to help with the words," the caretaker mewled. "An anachronism, but all that may be available to you, without the Interfaces. I can give you her location."

"Fine," Dawes growled, clenching his fingers into a fist. "Just send the data to my speeder port. And get me whatever you can about everything else. Soon, or I'll know who to blame when I get scolded. Goodbye, Citizen." The thought of being scolded by the head of K.C. must have been too much for the caretaker. He hurried to enter the data into his screen and nodded to indicate it had been done. Unable to resist one last look at the people integrated with the computers of the Republic, Dawes shuddered and stalked out of Interface Offices. He was glad that he hadn't been considered intelligent enough to be Placed as an Interface. Everyone had their Place in the Republic. He was glad that wasn't his.

The address Dawes's speeder took him to was connected, technically, to the research laboratories of Kyper University. The display of his speeder told him quite clearly, though, that "Tongues and Texts" was unaffiliated with the University, except for access to ancient documents or students for research. The fact that the building was attached to the labs was comforting to Dawes. No one was allowed near the labs unless they were visiting on a tour prior to Placement, were part of the research, part of the government, or they worked there. To be attached to the labs gave this person, whoever she was, at least a modicum of credence.

Dawes stepped up to the building and was granted admission, the security-drones recognising his status and position within K.C. He stepped inside and was transported to a world he thought only existed in the archives of the Republic. For one, there were no computers. At least, none that he could see. The only sign of technology, as he knew it, was the security system. Everything else was…well, he didn't quite know how to describe it.

There were books—he recognised those from a fieldtrip he had taken to the archives many years ago, before his Placement—on shelves around the walls. There was a table in the centre of the room with chairs arranged precisely. Two of the walls were filled with black panels covered in writings he couldn't recognise. One of the black panels had the words, *Nehrun tai hanen* written on them in large, clear font. Immediately, Dawes reached for his stun-gun and searched for the person who had written them.

She was standing in the far corner of the room perfectly still, staring at him, eyes wide, the page of the book she was holding still suspended between two fingers. Dawes pointed the stun-gun at her, and she yelped—actually yelped—before dropping the book and raising her hands into the air. Dawes wanted to get a good look at her before he shot. She was of average height, average beauty, though her skin displayed the slightly darker tones of the Carthinian Islands. Her hair was brown and tied up in a messy knot. She wore standard citizen clothing – tunic, leggings, all in a deep blue. Nothing special. Dawes wouldn't have paid any attention to her were she in a crowd, but as she was the only one in the room, it was impossible not to notice her.

"You are under arrest for crimes against the Republic, as evidenced by the writing on that wall," Dawes said, snapping out the words before his official greeting so she wouldn't have time to think. Or run.

The woman raised her brow and pointed to the words. "*That?* I didn't—I mean, that's not. I'm a linguist, not a terrorist!" she practically cried.

Dawes hesitated, something he did not often do. It was something in the absolute shock in her words, maybe. He didn't know what it was, but he hesitated.

"Linguist?" he asked. Was that like an Interface? The caretaker *had* sent him here.

"Yes. Linguists study language. Break them down into their pieces, sounds, grammar, things like that. And we look at how people use language based on different cultures and social settings and…Look, I'm just studying the words. After they were broadcast over every screen in Kyper, I couldn't resist," she explained.

Dawes narrowed his eyes. "Why would you bother studying

something like that. That's what Interfaces are for," Dawes growled.

"Sort of, yes. I mean, they *can* look at it, but it's not quite the same. Have you ever known an Interface to translate sarcasm? Or explain the difference between language used when talking with a superior versus someone you don't know? Or even look at how Common has evolved?"

Dawes considered and concluded she did have a point. He holstered his stun-gun, though it was clear he would happily pull it out again if the need arose. Dawes was looking at the first person to have an admitted fascination with the words. The Interfaces knew nothing. This was his only chance. But she was nothing more than an unobtrusive nobody, a Citizen without distinction. She was barely old enough to have come out of Kyper University, let alone be the "expert" that might help him figure out what was going on with these words.

"So, you do that? I mean, you study language?"

"Yes. I look at the patterns in a way the Interfaces, well, can't," she relaxed her stance and picked up the book, smoothing out wrinkled pages, and put it back on the shelf behind her.

Dawes snorted and shook his head. "I doubt you can do something that the Interfaces can't. They're human minds enhanced by the most advanced computer technology out there," Dawes pointed out.

She raised her brow again; this time in a skeptical gesture rather than shocked. "Or are they computers enhanced by human minds?" she said.

Dawes frowned. "It's all about how you phrase things, which, by the way, is also something I examine."

She bordered on impertinence. Dawes found himself giving her grudging respect for that. Not many people were willing to be impertinent with the lawmen of the Republic. They had too much power for that. Most people, those of lower Placements, shuddered and trembled in the presence of an Inspector for Kyper Central. The people of higher Placements made the laws. This one, though, had moxy. He wasn't sure he liked her, or trusted her, but she may be his best option. Maybe his *only* option.

"Inspector Maddox Dawes, Kyper Central," he said, holding out his hand.

She crossed the room and took it, her grip soft but firm.

"Amaia Wainright," she replied. "I take it you're here about those words."

Straight to business, good. "The K.C. Interfaces have no information whatsoever on those words. Five incidents, plus the attack last night, and they have nothing. Do you know how impossible that is?"

"Five incidents?" Amaia widened her eyes and leaned against the table. "Why haven't we heard about—"

"Because citizens have no need to know the actions of dissidents. The spreading of terror is the only way the dissidents have a voice, so we limit it." Dawes realised too late that he had given her information he should have been keeping close to the chest. A simple question and he was all but handing her the case file. If she had the information and the Interfaces truly couldn't help, then that was fairly inevitable. There was protocol to follow, though, and he hadn't. He hadn't even given the official greeting, informing this person that he was here with the authority of the Republic behind him. He knew precisely what Daleni Itar would say, and it wouldn't be good. This was a high-profile case; he couldn't afford to make mistakes. "It doesn't matter that you've never heard of it," Dawes growled, "all I need to know is whether or not you can tell me what those words mean."

Amaia nodded in consideration and stepped towards the papers strewn over the table. Dawes followed, noting that there was nothing intelligible on them: charts that made no sense, symbols that had no relation to Common as far as he could tell. The only thing he recognised were drawings of people, and even those were done in a blocky, strange style that looked simplistic and old at the same time. If this was what this "linguist" did, then she could have it.

"Well, it's difficult to work with only one sample and no other referents, but near as I can tell, the language it comes from is old."

"Old"? Dawes knew of no other language in Republic history apart from some earlier forms of Common. He knew that there had to have been a time when most of the nations had their own languages, but it was easier for everyone to speak Common. The Republic united everyone, gave them purpose and order. Anything before that—where people mingled with anybody and had no set purpose, where they fell victim to violence, famine, and war—was long ago lost to legend and nightmare-inducing tales told to children.

Amaia gestured to a collection of symbols laid out in rows. "This alphabet? It doesn't belong to any of the known languages of the early days of the Republic. I examined some ancient documents in the University archive and found something similar, though of course it's impossible to say exactly—"

"Why?" Dawes snapped. He needed exact.

"Because the language I found is old enough that there wouldn't be anyone who even remembers that it existed, let alone can translate it. Pre-Republic era," Amaia said, her voice reverent.

Dawes curled a lip. "There is nothing pre-Republic," he said firmly.

Amaia startled him by raising a single skeptical eyebrow but said nothing. She obviously disdained that notion, and expressing that to one of the higher officers of the Republic didn't frighten her at all.

Dawes stared at her until she looked away, colour rising in her face.

"Something had to exist pre-Republic. How could people have formed separate nations if there was nothing pre-Republic," she said quietly. She shook her head and touched the sheet again. "It doesn't matter. This language is old. I don't know much about it except that it's called Eloaech and is said to have been used by the original inhabitants of Taloria, called the Eloai. I think it means…wanderers? Strangers? Travellers? Something like that."

"So, you know what the language is." Dawes nodded, satisfied. This data could be handed to the Interfaces and they could compile it and discover who was using it now. The reason they didn't know anything about it was because it was old enough to be before recorded Republic history and the ancient documents were only beginning to be uploaded into the Interfaces.

Amaia shook her head. "Maybe. I've found a few words of Eloaech and they sound, and look, as though it could be from the same language, but there is a huge margin for error at this point. I don't have enough data. Just finding what I have was nearly impossible. Those documents were half-buried under some rubble in a collapsed storage cellar. I found them ages ago and still hardly have a grasp on the language. Then, well, the incident with the screen happened, and I pulled the documents out again," she said. "And I have no idea what any of it means."

"It doesn't matter what you know," Dawes said, gathering up the papers on the table. "I'll supply the information to the Interfaces and get this sorted out before there are any more incidents."

Amaia frowned. "If they didn't have information on this before, what makes you think that the Interfaces will discover something new now"?

Did he really have to explain these things to her? "Because they are the best, and because they have all records of the Republic at their fingertips." Dawes shoved the papers under his arm and held out his hand, which Amaia took, though she didn't seem pleased about the matter. "Thank you for your assistance," Dawes said.

"Please bring those back as soon as you're finished with them," Amaia said, her eyes pleading silently with him. "I'd like to do more research."

Dawes gave a noncommittal shrug and walked out. He didn't know why she would need such things, but it hardly mattered. This whole mess would soon be over.

3

The room was unobtrusive and average, nothing more than the middling level quarters the Republic gave to all single people of average Placement. There was a bed, desk, bureau, and closet, small kitchen off a nook, bathroom, and a small sitting area. There was nothing remarkable about the room excepting that it was dark but for the glow of the computer display. A figure sat before the display, fingers weaving through the air with expert efficiency, a gloved hand sending signals to the computer to match the fine electrical impulses of the person's skin. Numbers, graphs, symbols, drawings, words flashed on the screen almost too quickly for the naked eye to see. Every now and again, the person paused, making a sound of consideration.

"Inspector Maddox Dawes," the person said, rolling the name around with curiosity. "The man assigned to take over my investigation. An impeccable record, if I do say so myself, and…my, my, nearly set to be Decommissioned. Everyone thinks they're prepared for that, but they rarely ever are."

The screen flickered for a few minutes more as the figure read through Dawes' files, pausing every now and again as something of interest was found. "You do have a certain, hmm, *devotion* to the

Republic, it would appear, Inspector," the figure mused. "And an almost blind trust in those beloved Interfaces, though your noted reactions says that you fear them, too. Well, well, what have we here? Twenty-three uses on cases in the last two years. It almost makes one wonder if you can think for yourself. I think we should find out."

With a flick of the wrist, the gloves pulsed a burst of information to the computer and the screen went dark for a moment before restarting. In an underground system of tunnels throughout the city, the people intertwined with the computers of the Republic let out a single cry, each voice blending to one until it could be heard through the ventilation system in the streets. People in speeders paused, trying to hone-in on the sound, while their counterparts on the pavement froze in shock. The computers of Kyper responded to the sound by sending a burst of electricity through the circuits, glowing brighter before going dark.

The figure in the room, computer dim but still glowing, watched the result with reassuring calm, the data moving rapidly on the screen the only indication that something had happened.

"Message to all of Kyper. Hello, Citizens," the person said, placid and collected, even when giving the official greeting of the Republic. *"Nehrun tai hanen. Hra skanun."*

4

"It's only words...unless they're true."
—David Mamet

"What do you mean the data is gone"? Dawes tried to keep his voice level, but he had never been known to control his temper. It was what made him so good at his job: his dogged determination, the fear everyone had of his rages and the official power behind them. The caretaker winced over the screen, licking his lips nervously.

"I mean that the data you gave to the Interfaces yesterday is gone. Nowhere in the system. And all mention of the…incidents, up to and including last night's attack, is also gone." Dawes curled his lip in disgust, and the caretaker took a shuddering breath. Dawes doubted the man would have been so brazen had they been speaking face to face. Dawes took three deep breaths, forcing his eyes unfocused so that he wouldn't see the caretaker's face and have to start all over. After he was done, he didn't feel any calmer, but there was a sense of purpose to his anger. He glared at the man on his display.

"And how did that happen?" Dawes asked, his voice sharp. The caretaker winced and shifted. He muttered something, his eyes darting to glance at something off screen. Dawes bared his teeth in what could loosely be called a grin. "What was that?" he asked.

"We were hacked," the caretaker burst out. "It's the only logical explanation. The Interfaces don't lose information. Unless someone *wants* it lost. But that would mean hacking the main core of the

Republic's repository and…well, that's impossible."

"Obviously, it's not," Dawes snarled.

"Yes, well, even so. The person who did this would have to have access to the most advanced CoreTech equipment, things that aren't even in production yet. And the skill would have to be…it would be on par with…some of the highest Placements in history. They would have to be able to—"

"Taking out the entire electrical grid to send a message over all of Kyper, say, twice"? Dawes didn't realise that he was clenching his teeth, still holding his feral grin. The caretaker squeaked and nodded.

"There is nothing I can do. I have to personally see to the health of the Interfaces affected, make certain that nothing else is missing," the caretaker breathed. "I can do nothing more to help you. Once I learn more about how this was done, you will be informed. Goodbye, Citizen."

The display vanished in a burst of holographic dust before Dawes had a chance to respond. He growled and rose, letting out a dull roar of frustration before slamming his fist into the wall. This time, he hit properly and didn't do any more damage than bruise his knuckles and break the skin. Good, he thought grimly. He didn't have any more nanites to heal him. They were illegal tech anyways, banned years ago once the first generation of test subjects had died. There were theories about the offspring of such unions bearing genetically enhanced nanites, but —this wasn't helping him at all. He was still furious, and now he had nothing more than a few pieces of paper with illegible scribblings and drawings that meant nothing to him. He was going to be killed, personally, by Daleni Itar if he didn't come up with something. Soon.

Dawes reached for the papers to fling them into the rubbish-incinerator and paused, stopping himself just in time. "Idiot," he snarled. He grabbed the papers in a haphazard pile and rushed out the door, ignoring Daleni Itar as she came down the hall.

"Greetings, Citizen! Inspector Dawes!" she called. Dawes kept moving. "Where are you going"?

"A lead," Dawes called over his shoulder, adding as a casual afterthought, "Citizen."

"You say that whoever was responsible for the blackouts the last two nights hacked the Republic computers and removed all mention of the language and the incidents"? Amaia poured out a cup of tea and handed it to Dawes.

He took it and sniffed at the dark liquid suspiciously. There seemed nothing to do but drink and wait for Amaia to tell him what he needed. The new words from the night before were on the black wall beside the originals:

Nehrun tai hanen. Hra skanun.

There were diagrams and scribblings pointing to different parts of the words, with other notations all around them in what looked like the same language, though Dawes couldn't tell for certain. It was a completely foreign concept to him, looking at something like this. And to do it without the Interfaces was…well, he wasn't terribly pleased to be relying on this nobody Placement of a girl—no matter how intelligent she seemed.

"Any closer to figuring out what it means"?

Dawes purposefully didn't answer her question, but something in her eyes told him that she didn't need his reply. The answer was obvious. She tightened her mouth into a straight line and shrugged, sipping at her own tea.

"The new words helped. Confirmed that I'm dealing with Eloaech, though the modern usage could be quite different from the ancient one. I can reasonably well tell you that the first word is an imperative. Um, that's about all at this stage. I'll need to spend more time researching to learn more."

"An imperative?"

"A command. In this case, probably a second-person command. If I were to tell you to jump, that would be similar," Amaia said. "It's… well, Common is derived from the most popular language spoken in the Republic before the rulers deemed it necessary to speak one language. That was Ionan. From what I understand, there were two major languages on Taloria, Myosian—that's about the Crepuscule area and north—and Eloaech, which was centred here. Eloaech developed into Ionan which became Common. In Common, the command 'jump' is a single verb with an implied but absent subject, 'you'."

"What does that have to do with *nehrun?*" *Where was she getting this information?* Dawes hadn't ever heard of such information regarding the origins of Common. And learning about imperatives and similar nonsense, well, frankly, who cared?

"If you look at the first phrase, you have three words, two of which end in 'un'. The second phrase is similar to *nehrun,* except for the first half. So I assume that *skanun* and *nehrun* are similar, probably meant to be conjugated verbs. In such a short sentence, it would make sense that they were verbs. And having only one other word in the second sentence would mean that the verb would likely be an imperative. Making *nehrun* also an imperative. And it's unlikely that someone hacking would send a message using anything other than the second-person imperative and…and you don't care, do you?" Amaia's skin coloured slightly, which brought a wry smile to Dawes' mouth.

"No. Not as long as you tell me what it means, I don't need to know how you came by the answers," Dawes said, frowning. "Though it seems unusual that you care so much. Why are you studying this… language nonsense to begin with? The Interfaces would do anything that needs to be done. That's what they do."

"Well, apparently not at the moment," Amaia said flatly.

Dawes grunted in frustrated agreement.

"I could have been an Interface. I was capable enough and the Placement exams all indicated that I would be perfect as an Interface or high-level studying to become a subject expert."

"Obviously, you chose subject expert." After seeing the Interfaces, Dawes wasn't terribly shocked at such a decision. He knew that it was an honour to be placed as an Interface, but the second option seemed a better one to him. Not everyone had such a terrible decision, though. He personally had been destined for Kyper Central his entire life. Which suited him fine. He was good at his job and had proudly served—if with great displays of temper—for his entire career. He wouldn't have done anything differently. Amaia, though, had been one of the unfortunate. She'd had a choice to burden her.

He wanted to push her, get her to tell him everything about the words. He needed to solve this case yesterday and this was straying too far from the subject. Dawes reminded himself that he had brought up her motives. *Her credentials,* he thought. *I am merely checking her credentials.*

She nodded. "I did," she said. "It was more appealing. And now I am helping you solve a terrible crime, so I think it's probably worth it."

"Were you Placed with a specific subject?" Dawes asked. If she was meant to do this, then he could turn the conversation back to the problem at hand. She shook her head, one corner of her mouth quirking mischievously, as if guessing his thoughts.

"No," she said. "I think it better that way. I got to choose what I wished to do, and the Placement exam was fine with that. I chose to do what no one else does and study languages. I am, as far as I know, the only linguist in the Republic."

"But if you *had* to choose," Dawes pushed, uncomprehending, "why language? What purpose does that serve? Engineering or Computers or Societal Management or even Government, you could have been a subject expert in any of those. You could have been recognised over the entire Republic. But no one knows who you are now. Everyone speaks Common and they don't need to speak anything else."

"You know, don't you?" Amaia asked, laughing.

It was a merry sound, which only served to confuse Dawes more. He didn't understand her at all. He ground his teeth and let out a slow breath through his nose. He needed answers.

"Why language? Why linguistics? What makes you qualified to help in this investigation?" Dawes said, unconsciously leaning forwards in his seat.

"Let me ask you a question, Inspector Dawes." She stood and walked to where she had written on the wall. He had other questions to answer, but if his instincts were right, then this average-looking girl dressed in the plain clothing of a subject-expert—barely old enough to claim being a woman—was going to be essential in his investigation. So he stopped and humoured her, grunting as an indication to continue.

"How do computers get information"?

"What?" he practically snarled. He was here to figure out what that stupid phrase meant, not discuss the mechanics of computers. If he even knew.

"I assure you, Inspector, the question is not a trick. It is relevant," she said, her eyes still fixed on the scene outside the window. He reminded himself that she was necessary. He still couldn't bring himself to answer the question. She looked at him and waited. Finally, he spoke.

"They transmit information," he grumbled.

"Yes, but how? It is not an instantaneous thing. Computers used to communicate through a series of zeroes and ones, a binary system telling a computer whether a circuit was on or off. An electrical impulse. They did not communicate without a human telling them to do so, however, so it could hardly be considered a living language. A set of instructions, perhaps even advanced pattern recognition. Yet now, with the advent of human integration and true artificial intelligence, computers communicate in a much more complex manner. Electrical impulses, yes, but they can be spoken by a human."

"What's the point of this?" Dawes asked. His patience was running thin. The woman turned to him and smiled. The light from the window framed her hair, masking her face in shadow.

"What is a language"?

Dawes curled his lip and thought, pulling out, "A means of communication."

Amaia smiled indulgently and shook her head. "Yes, and no. Animals communicate, and yet they do not have language. A language is learned. It is, as you said, a means of communication, but it is communication by means of symbols. A computer's binary language symbolises what people want computers to do. The words I'm speaking represent a concept or an idea or an emotion. The clothes I wear—the uniforms that everyone wears—are a symbol and act as part of non-verbal communication. They tell you I am a subject-expert, a Citizen, attached to the University. My facial expressions and body movements tell you when I'm happy, frustrated, interested. It is intentional, voluntary, and also involuntary, subconscious. Many people do not think about their word choice, which tells me how their subconscious translates their identity into language."

"And you study all of that"? The topic, now that Amaia had illustrated it, seemed more than immense.

"Much of it, yes," Amaia nodded. "Think about the language you would use with a Konsular as opposed to a Cook. Would it be different?"

"Yes, of course," Dawes said. She was asking obvious questions, now. He didn't need the obvious, he needed to understand this dissident language.

"Why"?

Dawes froze, mind running through a number of possible explanations. He came up with only, "They're just different people, is all."

"One has a higher relative position than you, the other lower. You can choose to approach a Cook, but a Cook cannot choose to approach you without a breach of the social system. Just in the same way that you cannot choose to approach a Konsular but must be summoned. They exist in entirely different spheres from you. Your language reflects that."

"That seems…absurd. The Placement system divides us, sure, but we're all Citizens of the Republic, no one greater or better. We're all provided for," Dawes defended, resisting the urge to hunch his shoulders.

"And yet you yourself admitted that you would speak to a Konsular differently than a Cook. But there is more than just the purpose of a speech act, there is also the structure and function of individual words or lexemes, morphemes: parts of a word that carry meaning, sounds or phonetics, grammar, or syntax. Someone trained to listen can determine if a person is from the Crepuscule area of the Republic, as opposed to Kyper, just by the way they speak Common. Words, symbols, language, it's everywhere, and it's hugely underestimated." Amaia nodded firmly, and Dawes had the distinctly unpleasant sensation of being technically superior in Placement but potentially inferior in intellect. He wasn't sure he liked it, but he wasn't sure he could manage the investigation without it.

Dawes went back to his flat with a feeling of disquiet. Talking with Amaia had been…well, he didn't know what it had been. He never cared what sort of words he was using, never thought about language like she seemed to. But now that she had pointed these things out, he couldn't *stop* thinking about it. As she said, it was everywhere.

"Message waiting," the voice of his computer told him as Dawes walked in, unbuttoning his jacket and letting out a long breath.

"Play," Dawes growled, trying to clear his mind.

"Dawes, I don't know what you think you're doing, but you had better come in with a lead tomorrow or you're going to be out of a job, and I'm going to be in front of the PressCams explaining why Kyper Central hasn't come up with a lead. My head's on the line for this one." Daleni Itar sounded displeased. Dawes growled again, this time wordlessly and continued listening, but that was the end of the message.

"Delete message." Dawes sank into his couch and propped up his feet. He felt more exhausted after talking today than he had in a while.

Probably due to his mind spinning around in circles. "No response." He ground the heels of his palms into his eyes and groaned. Daleni Itar was unlikely to take his progress today as a good sign. Sure, he knew the name of the language and that one, or maybe two, of the words were imperatives. That didn't actually help him get anywhere near solving this mystery, though. And Amaia needed more information before she could tell him anything further regarding the words.

Which left only the Dreamscape.

How could Dawes have forgotten? The Dreamscape was the only forensic evidence that had been recovered from the theft sites. The pilots and their crews didn't remember anything, but perhaps the actual drug could provide information. *Enough to lead him somewhere?* Dawes wasn't sure, but it was all he had. Better use that information or his head was going to be on the line. Decommissioning? Unlikely. He'd be roasted alive if he couldn't come up with something worthwhile.

"Computer, contact the lab processing the Dreamscape. Tell them I want a report. Now. Or their heads are going to be served up to my superiors." Dawes leaned his head back and closed his eyes.

5

The girl, young, dark-skinned and too thin, stepped lightly between buildings. The drones swept overhead, but she timed her movements for when they were looking the other way. It was almost too easy; she grinned to herself. The Republic, so secure, so safe, convinced that they could prevent anything.

What fools they were.

Skiya knew better. She had been on the streets of Kyper since she was old enough to run away from her family. She had been six, maybe seven-years-old. She wasn't certain. She didn't care.

Down here, on the ground level in the heart of Kyper, things were different. This wasn't higher up, where the Konsulars, CoreTech workers and the higher-ups lived. They were fine to stay up there and look out on the vast expanse of the city. Down here, the structure and protection of the Republic mattered less. Real light rarely managed to breach this far. And even the security forces hated coming down here. That was why they sent drones to monitor the lowlifes.

Lowlifes. Skiya smirked as she jumped into an alleyway just before a drone passed by. It was struggling along, one of its wing-shielded propellers bent. Someone must have managed to hit it with a rock. They were likely on the wanted lists now for wanton and rebellious destruction of Republic property.

Good luck finding them. This was where the life happened, Skiya knew. Not up above. Not in the pretty gardens that the Republic cultivated for the illusion of life and nature. Not in the offices of the Placed workers who would likely never interact with the people in the building next to them. The real people lived down on the ground.

They were the ones who weren't upset when the Republic forgot about them.

"Interesting," Skiya murmured, catching sight of a clean, well-cut coat. It's tan colour and quality tailoring was enough to make it seem out of place. Along with the silver-haired straight-back who wore it, she was seeing something that didn't often happen at Ground Level. He turned enough for Skiya to catch a glimpse of silver on his lapel.

Skiya hissed and pressed back against the building, glad for her dark clothes and dark skin. She didn't want to get in the lawman's sights. The people who lived down here weren't often noticed by the Republic, but that didn't mean they weren't aware of the power the Republic held. After all, it was the Republic that made certain the rest of the Citizens didn't even know they lived down here. It was all too easy for them to be removed and forgotten.

"I'm not going to wait forever," the lawman growled. Skiya peeked out from the corner and watched. He wasn't talking to her. Across the street, one of the forgotten people crawled out. She looked a mess but she was doing better than some. Her clothes—all cast-offs—were smeared with grime, but they were whole. Her hair was short, probably hacked off for easy bartering. Her skin was pale from lack of light. She moved with this sort of twitching, stop-and-go motion. Her eyes, though, were glassy, heavy, and distant.

A Dreamscape user, Skiya noted. There weren't all that many down here. Dreamscape wasn't impossible to get, but it was difficult enough. If the Republic officials got one whiff of the drug being used, they came down like a swarm of wasps and erased it—as well as all connection to it—from existence. The regular Citizens probably didn't even know the drug was still available, let alone used. But it was. Just not by people on Upper Levels.

"Inspector," the woman purred, her voice more sultry than her appearance let on. She reached out to touch the lawman and he snatched her wrist out of the air.

"Please don't," the lawman said with obvious distaste, "I've already bathed today, Nathalia, and I wouldn't want to waste more of the Republic's resources."

"Oh, such a shame. I wouldn't want to ruin your impeccable appearance," Nathalia said, an easy smile on her face. You'd have thought she was talking to a good friend, for all the pleasure she showed. Skiya spit on the ground.

"You're all doped up," the lawman said. "So, you found a new supply."

"You were kind enough to let me go after my last dealer got raided," Nathalia simpered. She batted her eyelashes, though the effect was ruined by the glassy stare. "Everyone knows how much you hate Dreamscape. Why would you let me go, Inspector?"

Why, indeed? Skiya thought, leaning a little farther out from the wall to better observe the scene. The drones swept by and Skiya retreated back again, grumbling quietly. The lawman and the Dreamscaper didn't even blink. Probably because the lawman wasn't in any danger of being spotted and because the Dreamscaper couldn't be bothered to consider the drones a threat.

"You know full why, Nathalia," the lawman snapped. "Because you were dumb enough to agree to a deal with me. I keep you away from the security forces, you get clean, and tell me where you get your supplies. Seems to me that you aren't keeping your end of the bargain."

"You got my last supplier," Nathalia protested, a whine creeping into her voice. "You can't expect me to do more than that."

"That's exactly what I expect," the lawman said. He took three deep breaths, jaw clenched. "Look, Nathalia, I've been handed a big case. Some stupid bash-and-dash turned into big news. It's got Dreamscape all wrapped up in this. And you're all wrapped up in Dreamscape, so I figure you can tell me what's what."

Nathalia made enough effort to glance over both shoulders. Skiya saw the barest hint of fear start to show itself on the Dreamscaper's face. Skiya bared her teeth; the drug was wearing off. Things could get dicey if that happened too quickly. She should just go on her way, leave the lawman and the Dreamscaper to their fates. But that would ruin all the fun. And what was the point of being your own master if you couldn't indulge your curiosity a bit? *Who in the Republic would care anyway?*

"Look, Inspector, I don't know what you're mixed up in," Nathalia began, taking exactly one step backwards.

The lawman's hand flashed out and he grabbed her arm.

"How about this," he said, voice calm and soothing, though there was an underlayment of temper. "I get you to a clinic. You know the Republic cares for all of its people. You get to a clinic, you get clean, you get back into your Placement. You'll get food, shelter, be with your own people—"

"I won't go back," Nathalia spat. Oh, yeah, the drug was definitely wearing off.

"Why"?

Skiya rolled her eyes. It was almost cute how the lawman seemed genuinely confused about why the Dreamscaper didn't want to go back into the fold. He obviously didn't understand what it was like, having the Republic look over your shoulder every day. The pressure to be a "good" citizen. Ha. As if most people even understood what was required of them in their Placement. They were nothing but a bunch of wide-eyed sheep being herded from one place to another. Eat this. Sleep now. Mine this. Build that.

Skiya wanted to explore, to learn. To paint. She wanted to *live*.

"I can't help you," Nathalia said, squirming from the lawman's grasp. She didn't run, though. She just glanced around again and rubbed her wrist—a nervous tick. "I don't know anything."

"You're holding out on me," the lawman snarled. He jabbed a finger at Nathalia. "You don't want to know what I can do to you when you hold out on me."

"No more than they can," Nathalia spat.

Skiya straightened, the muscles in her shoulders tensing. A Dreamscaper wouldn't know much, but they might know enough. Enough to give a hint.

"They? Your dealers? Come on, Nathalia, give me something," the lawman hissed.

"It's bigger than you," Nathalia spat, holding her hands close to her chest.

"Who is it? Who's dealing?"

"The ones who know how things are really going to end up," Nathalia said. "The ones who know what it means to be trapped."

The lawman swiped a hand through his hair, fury etching itself in the lines on his face. "I'm trying to be reasonable. But I've had a hell of a day. That nonsense language that they've been showing about, the Dreamscape that you..." he trailed off, peering closely at Nathalia's face. "You think they're connected."

"I don't know anything," the Dreamscaper insisted. She tried to step around the lawman, but he held out an arm and she stepped back. Stuck.

"Nathalia, the Republic isn't going to hurt you. We just want to get you somewhere safe, out of the cold. I don't know why you're so upset. You could have everything you need. A place to live, clothes, food. None of this living rough. You could have a purpose in life," the lawman tried to plead.

Skiya shook her head.

He really didn't get it.

Nathalia was coming out of the haze of the drug; she looked at the lawman with distaste. And fear. "I can't tell you anything. It's dangerous."

"Dangerous? Why?"

Nathalia flicked her eyes over the streets. Skiya stayed perfectly still so her movement wouldn't reveal her position. She could hear a drone heading back in their direction. A bead of sweat ran down the back of her neck. Being caught on a drone camera wasn't a death sentence, but it was bad enough. She was a runaway. Still a youth, by Republic standards. She really hated getting caught on camera.

The Dreamscaper licked her lips, speaking in a whisper, "Those words that appeared on all the screens? That's why."

This time, when Nathalia ran, the lawman didn't stop her. The drone followed the Dreamscaper with dogged interest. Skiya slipped back another few feet as the pair passed by. Nathalia ran for all she was worth and eventually managed to slide into the shadows where the drone didn't bother following. Why should it, when it had a beat on her now?

A whole city of drones with a central database could map a person's movements—and criminal history—within an hour. Just one glimpse of you could be enough and…the Republic would *have* to bring you back into the fold. Or send you to the Rabesh colony. Skiya wasn't certain which was worse.

The behemoth that was the Republic may have looked all shiny and enticing to some. But Skiya knew full well that the people within the Republic's system rarely questioned their purpose in life. They were given everything they thought they could need. That was the trick. The Republic choked out everything that wasn't aligned with their ideals. Slowly, the people's thoughts about what they needed were be lessened. Their questions silenced. The Republic was mother and father and eternal.

Skiya shivered involuntarily. She clenched her jaw at the reaction, hating that the Republic still had that much pull over her emotions. Soon, though, things would be different. The Citizens would see that the Republic was anything but eternal and all-encompassing.

She had once asked her parents what was before the Republic, whether there had been people who understood the mysteries of the universe. Because it seemed that the Republic was trying to teach them how to be productive in their Placement, how to be a good and fruitful Citizen, when Skiya just wanted to know what caused the seasons. Or what lay beyond the moon colony and the stars. Why they all ate meat but never saw the animals. What it felt like to swim in an ocean. How to put the vibrant blue midnight she had once viewed on a trip to the top of the city's buildings at sunset onto paper.

Skiya had been soundly beaten for her impertinence. The security forces in the observation dome had watched in silence.

"We are not Placed to ask foolish questions. Those at the top, the

Konsulars, the Head of the Republic—they have the answers to all the questions, and if we need to know more, the Republic will tell us," her mother had said.

"Then I want to talk with one of the Konsulars," Skiya had replied, her jaw stiff from the blows. The slap her father had dealt knocked her backwards. She hit her head on the glass window, making the pain in her jaw and ribs feel like a pleasant breeze by comparison. Her mother had looked away, features schooled and blank.

Skiya had run away soon after.

A pair of drones crossed paths overhead, slowing for an instant as they exchanged data. Skiya kept hidden in the darkness of a sheltered door, just outside of view. The drones sped on and the young girl grinned wolfishly. She slipped through the streets, moving towards her home. To the place where the people the Republic had abandoned would gather. To the people who were more family to her than any memory of those that had borne her.

The best part was that the Republic had no idea of any of it.

6

"**M**essage from lab," the computer said smoothly after a few minutes. Message reads:

Greetings, Citizen.

Data available.

Please come to lab for discussion.

"Why would they want me to come there?" Dawes hissed. But he was already standing. He tipped back the last few drops of his drink and closed his eyes. Talking with Nathalia had been a disgusting but necessary move. Dawes hated the Ground Level. There were people there who had no idea of the purpose of the Republic. They scorned safety and comfort, and for what? Drugs, mostly.

"Unknown. Should I query?" the computer asked.

He snarled an expletive and stalked to the speeder bay. It was late. He was tired. But at least this was something. The speeder did all the work, which left Dawes time to think. Maybe the Dreamscape was part of the message. Nathalia had confirmed that the person responsible for blacking out the screen was the new Dreamscape dealer. Maybe even manufacturer, if this dissident was smart enough. And Amaia had said that language was more than just words and letters, but a whole collection of things. Body movements, arrangement of space. Could doping someone with Dreamscape be significant? More than just using the resources at hand, that is.

"Call Amaia Wainright," Dawes said. There was a pause and a few rings before she answered, her eyes tired and her hair slightly dishevelled, as if she had been sleeping, though she still wore her Subject-expert tunic and trousers.

"Inspector," Amaia said. Here brow raised with surprise while her mouth tightened in frustration at being awoken. "Has something happened? Did you get another message?"

Dawes shook his head. "No. I'm going to the lab to hear about the Dreamscape and wanted to know if the use of Dreamscape was part of a message. Could it be part of this language or the…use of language that you were talking about earlier?"

Amaia frowned, drawing her lips together as she thought. "Maybe. Perhaps. I could certainly have a look at the data and put together a profile of someone who would use it in such a circumstance. That's getting into more of the psychology area than I tend to work in, but the pragmatic use of drugs and other mind-altering substances has shown a tendency to change the way people use language, certainly. The *use* of Dreamscape in this circumstance may be a statement as well."

"Good. I'll meet you at the lab. I'm sending you the location now." Dawes ended the call before she had a chance to argue, or even give the appropriate farewell. He didn't have time to wait for her to look at the data he would send to her. He needed answers tonight. Besides, sometimes another perspective could be useful.

Dawes was mildly surprised to see Amaia already at the lab when his speeder arrived. She looked as professional as she had during the day, despite being dishevelled earlier, and some part of him admired her for that. Professionalism was essential. She waved as he disembarked his speeder. "They wouldn't let me inside to wait without you," she said.

Dawes walked to the door and it opened, his credentials getting him through as they did with everything else. "It helps being part of K.C. You get access to just about anywhere," Dawes said.

"Useful trick," Amaia commented. They were greeted by a lab technician who looked half-starved for a decent night's sleep. Dawes knew he should have felt remorse for keeping the woman there so late, working to grab at any desperate clue, but he didn't. His job—worse, his reputation and duty to the Republic—was on the line, and he didn't care who was standing in his way. Jobs from K.C. took precedence… over just about everything.

"Citizen. What was so important that you couldn't have just beamed me the data?" Dawes growled. The lab tech widened her eyes and gestured to Dawes and Amaia before turning and scurrying through a door. Beyond the door was what one would expect of a lab: computer terminals, testing equipment, microscopes, even beakers and tubes with various substances. Then there was the man standing off to one side and looking extremely displeased. He wore a dark grey tunic and breeches, both of the highest quality synthetics. His dark hair was slicked back, his caramel skin glowing with health stimulants. Dawes felt a familiar feeling of dislike and resentment rising in him, barely managing to swallow back a snarl of displeasure. "A Konsular," he sniffed instead.

Amaia made an inquisitive sound, self-consciously tugging at the everyman-blue of her own tunic. "Why?" she asked.

The Konsular pressed his lips together in disdain and gave a melodramatic sigh, obviously displeased to be in the lab at odd hours. The tech mumbled something and dashed to the microscope terminal, waving her hands. A substance appeared on the holoscreen, magnified by a considerable amount. "This is why," she said. At the confused looks of both Dawes and Amaia, plus one nervous glance at the silent Konsular, she continued, "This is the Dreamscape recovered from the bloodstreams of the victims. Each of the attacks contained the same composition. It's…there is nothing uncommon about it. The ingredients are nothing special. Except the, uh, chemical composition has a very unique signature."

She fell silent, her eyes flicking to the Konsular for a moment before settling firmly on the ground. Dawes turned expectantly to the man and hoped that he wouldn't have to coerce the man into saying anything. Kyper Central offered its Inspectors a lot of authority, but when it came to an all-out power battle between Konsulars and Inspectors, the Konsulars won more often than not. Inspectors were meant to have free reign to keep the people of the Republic out of crime. People, Dawes had been told by an irate instructor many years ago, were not Konsulars.

This Konsular curled his lip at Amaia, "I agreed to discuss the matter with the Inspector, not this…"

"This *Citizen*," Amaia began, her expression hardening into the sarcastic snarl that had so impressed Dawes. He doubted very much that the Konsular would be impressed by such tactics. "…is a member of the Republic and—"

"She is essential to the investigation," Dawes said flatly. "Hello, Citizen. May I introduce Amaia Wainright, the only linguist in the Republic, and as such, the person most likely to figure out what the words that were displayed across every holoscreen in the city mean. The Dreamscape may be a crucial piece of the message that these dissidents are trying to send, hence my reason for inviting her along."

"Surely there are other means—"

"There are not," Dawes interrupted the grey-clothed man and knew that, had his Decommissioning not been in a couple of months, his career would be over. Even now, the Konsular had enough power to make his life very, very difficult.

The man sniffed disdainfully and lifted his chin, eyeing Amaia. He coughed in the back of his throat, "Very well. The chemical composition of the Dreamscape matches the unique signature associated with the Dreamscape that is given to Konsulars and members of the Tech-Elite."

"What?" Dawes barely managed to hiss the word, and this time, it was Amaia who covered for him.

"Why would the Konsulars and Tech-Elite be issued Dreamscape? I thought the substance was illegal." She made it sound an innocuous question, completely innocent of anything but pure curiosity. As a result, the Konsular merely scoffed at her ignorance rather than her insinuation.

"Are you aware of the effects of Dreamscape"? The man turned to the lab-tech, who was watching the exchange with wide, terrified eyes. She hunched her shoulders slightly, the lab coat making her appear disfigured, and spoke as if reciting a formula.

"Dreamscape is a narcotic-type drug that alters the chemistry of the brain in order to enhance the chemicals associated with positive feelings. Happiness, relaxation, hope, agreeableness, trust, even love, are all enhanced while the negative feelings are dampened. It has no known effect on intelligence or focus, and the only known side-effects are an addiction to the altered perception of reality."

"Indeed," the Konsular turned away from the woman, who immediately went back to standing passively in the corner. Dawes remained silent, but he doubted the lack of other side-effects and the belief that there were no negative consequences while on the drug. Drugs were, by definition, something that was only taken when a person could no longer cope with reality and thereby admitted defeat and became a traitor to the Republic, to the world that was provided. Yet here was one of the top tier members of the Republic, Placed into his position by virtue of his intelligence, charisma, and Republic-knows-what-else, claiming that the Konsulars and Tech-Elite were *issued* Dreamscape.

"But that doesn't explain—" Amaia began again.

"We are Placed into our positions and given very specialised training. There is no one else in the Republic who understands the world in the way that we do. As a result, dealing with people outside of the Konsular and Tech-Elite Placements is extremely aggravating. In order to maintain a balance, and understand the reality of lower placements, we require Dreamscape. It allows us to understand multiple perspectives, and therefore make the Republic a more efficient, functional place for all its citizens." The Konsular's speech was cool and precise, with no hint of the shame that Dawes would have expected from a drug-user.

"So the Dreamscape used in the attacks was the same that is issued to you," Amaia said. Before the Konsular even had a chance to nod, she was moving to the computer terminal and waving her hands to write the words *Nehrun tai hanen + Dreamscape*. The words floated in the holoscreen, turning slowly. "It's a challenge," she said, eyes glinting with the success of realisation. "I mean a direct challenge, a message, to the ruling elite of the Republic. Whatever those words mean, the fact that the Dreamscape was directly linked to the Konsulars and Tech-Elite means that the message is pointed at them. These people, whoever they are, are not just chaos seekers," Amaia said, looking solely at Dawes.

He nodded, feeling a sinking feeling in the pit of his stomach. Not only was the Dreamscape connected to the Konsulars and Tech-Elite, but it was dealt by the dissidents who wrote the message. The Konsulars were dependent on this person or people. Dawes' mouth became dry and he licked his lips in a futile attempt to relieve some of the burden.

"They're attacking the foundation of the Republic."

7

The room was crowded with people. It was underground and windowless, with only artificial light giving off a gleam of life. The people moving restlessly under the light looked nervous, as if they were unused to even that gleam. The room was clean and bare of any furniture but for a few empty metal crates used as makeshift stools, and a single table at the far end of the room. No one approached the table.

People clustered in groups, murmuring to those they knew and eyeing those they didn't with open curiosity. They wore a variety of different clothing—from the uniforms of the youth teachers to the ragged clothing that was signature to those who lived on the run from the Republic authorities. No one seemed to care what clothing—or what office the clothing signified—people wore or if their skin betrayed their heritage as someone from Jushpe or Sazhem, nor if they were male or female. They were all there, strangers, or known associates, waiting. Most were tense, but they were all waiting.

"Nehrun tai hanen, my friends," one person said, standing on the table. The murmuring died down and everyone turned to stare at this person. They watched with hungry gazes, eager and desperate alike.

"Hra skanun," some of the people replied. Those who hadn't spoken merely stared, as if unknowing or unable to speak.

"The tenets of the Eloai have served us well, have they not?" the speaker said. At those words, there was some murmuring. The speaker grinned, eyes flashing in the flickering lights. "I see we have some people who do not yet understand. Yet you are here, so you must understand something."

"Unless there are spies," the young, dark-skinned girl sneered.

The speaker looked down at the girl and gave a shake of the head.

"Hush, Skiya. If they are curious, who am I to deny them knowledge? After all, the seeking of knowledge is precisely why we are here." The speaker's attention shifted expertly from Skiya and it became clear, once again, that the entire audience was being addressed. Some people leaned forwards eagerly, giving the speaker their undivided attention, just as the speaker focused on them. "We are here to choose, my friends. We are here to uphold the principles of the Eloai, the Wanderers, and all that they represent. They did not place people into categories based on a test of the blood, but on skill and choice. They did not push people into certain relationships based on the characteristics they wanted to enhance, but on caring and community. They sought out knowledge, not to keep it hidden. They listened to people of all different creeds, reserving judgement until all information was gathered. They wandered and sought to understand. And above all else, they valued *freedom*."

That word, whispered though it was, rang through the room like a cry. A challenge of battle, daring anyone who opposed it to speak up. No one dared face that word, nor the fierce gleam in the eye of the speaker.

"Freedom," the speaker continued. "Do you know what it means"?

"The ability to live in peace from conflict due to things that we could not possibly prevent if there were no structure, as we are ignorant and subject to our own selfish desires," a man spoke this time, though he sat near Skiya. The speaker laughed through the nose and shared an amused glance with the man. Some of the other people in the room seemed to genuinely agree with his words, and their murmurs of agreement rolled through the crowd slowly.

"Devar, you have been reading the wrong dictionary," the speaker laughed. The man crossed his arms and chuckled as well. His grim facial features looked harsh with laughter, and his deep-grey and black rags seemed to take on a purposeful power. He fixed his eyes on the people nearest; they shuddered at the intensity of his reaction. The initial murmurs of agreement were abruptly silenced; instead, shock emanated from the people.

"Yes, friends, I know that those words are so enticing. They give the promise of *peace* from conflict. Of *happiness* without strife. But I ask you to consider one thing. Whose idea of peace and happiness is that? Did you choose that meaning or was it forced upon you as truth? Freedom: the original, true meaning of the word is the ability to decide for yourself who you are going to be, what you are going to do. Not what the Republic says you are going to do, because it will 'prevent conflict and ensure peace.' With that definition, you have no chance to even consider the fact that there might be something better!"

Outraged hisses flowed from the people to the speaker who nodded in agreement. "I know that many of you would not be here if you did not feel a sense of discontent with the way things are. The Republic tells you that you have no reason to be discontented. That you are exactly where you are meant to be. The truth of things is that you did not choose that. It was forced upon you. And what of those of us who do not choose? Look at Devar," the speaker gestured to the man.

He shifted and tightened his mouth into a line of silence, letting the speaker say his words for him.

"Devar was Placed into the role of Medic. He was trained and did his job well, until one of the emergencies he was trying to prevent—a woman electrocuted in her role of Engineer—died. The pain of that experience was so anguishing that Devar did not speak for nearly three months. The Republic did not care for his so-called 'pain', but demanded that he continue working. He did, until he couldn't take any more. Devar went to ground and has been living on the streets. A man who saved lives—until he couldn't—is now an outcast, spat upon when someone passes him because he did not conform to the Republic's whims. He didn't choose to become a Medic. He could have chosen a different role, a different path. But his freedom was taken from him."

Skiya shifted to lean a friendly shoulder against Devar, but her eyes were fixed on the speaker.

"Choice. Freedom. The seeking of knowledge. And a community built around such tenets, where people care for one another without being forced to do so. That is what we are trying to build. Are we going to let the Republic stop us?"

There was silence for a moment as the speaker's words sank in. Then someone shook their head, and another said, softly, "No." The phrase grew louder until it filled the room.

The speaker nodded and held up a hand. "I agree. The Republic calls us dissidents. Rebels. Rogues, even. But we are merely trying to be heard. I say to you, join me. Join the call for freedom. *Nehrun tai hanen. Hra skanun!*"

"*Nehrun tai hanen. Hra skanun!*" Skiya and Devar and a few others echoed, taking up the cry.

"Nehrun! Nehrun! Nehrun!"

The speaker nodded and smiled, pleased.

8

Dawes threw a book aside, not caring that it landed on its pages, bending a few, the spine breaking.

Amaia huffed and picked up the book, smoothing out the pages and frowning over the spine. She looked at Dawes with quiet accusation in her eyes.

He turned back towards the pile on the table with a grimace. "We've been at this for hours," Dawes said, "and we've only come up with a few references to the Eloai or Eloaech or anything. I don't know how you do anything without computers or Interfaces."

"I don't *not* use computers," Amaia corrected, replacing the book on the table and spreading her hands over a sheaf of papers in front of her. "It just so happens that, in this circumstance, not using them is more useful. I still don't understand how your rebels managed to remove all information about anything close to the subject from the database."

"That makes you and everyone else," Dawes hissed.

"Well, I was going to tell you that I had found something, before you threw my book." The linguist stood and moved to the wall with the writing, rubbing her hand over some pieces to clear them away. She wrote out, in a precise hand, *Eloai myor tlel hanun*. Never before had words made Dawes' head start spinning or his heart start beating faster, but at the sight of those, he practically salivated.

"You found something," he breathed, standing to go take a closer look at the words, as if they could just spring to life and solve all his problems right there. "I suppose you don't know what it means."

"Actually," Amaia turned the book she was holding to him and pointed to the unintelligible scrawl, "it says. Right here."

"What"?! Dawes snatched the book and pressed it close to his face, trying to read.

"*Eloai myor tlel hanun,*" Amaia recited, "Wanderer, stand here as witness."

"Is that good?" Dawes asked. It sounded significant, but it was from a book, not exactly what his rebels had said. Still, some things sounded similar. Or maybe that was just his imagination. He had only just started paying attention to the words around him a day or so ago. Amaia was the expert.

"Very good." She turned to him and flashed a grin. "Look at *hanun*. It's very likely that's a variant of *hanen*. Probably a different conjugation. I would imagine that it's probably a second person formal imperative, just like *nehrun*. And the words, what they mean, it's fantastic. *Eloai* is wanderer, obviously—"

"Oh, obviously," Dawes muttered, but he was excited, also.

Amaia shot him a wry glance. "Yes, obviously. And *hanun* being the verb, must be stand. It's a different word order than I expected, with the subject at the beginning and the verb at the end, rather than Common, which has the subject then the verb then the object. If that holds true, then *myor tlel* must either mean witness as or as witness. Based on the inverted word order, I would guess that *myor* is witness— probably with conjugation—and *tlel* must be as."

"You got all of the that from a single sentence"? Dawes was impressed.

"Yes, but the interesting bit is that I can tell you more about the words the hacker used. *Nehrun tai hanen.*"

"You can? Does the book say more about—"

"It does. *Hanen,* we know, is an imperative. Stand. Here, the book gives some phrases with personal pronouns. *Tai* is us. And there are forms—nominal forms—of *Nehrun,* in circumstances of being called forth in solving disputes, which is where the Wanderer as witness piece comes in. *Nehrun.* See, watch, observe. Put all of that together and you get 'Watch us stand'." Amaia fingered the pages of the book before looking up at Dawes. Her words had been quick, strung together, as if she couldn't get them out fast enough. Dawes took a moment longer, revelling in the sense of fierce pleasure that came from figuring something out. He bared his teeth at Amaia in a semblance of a grin, and something sparked in her eyes in result.

"We have them," Dawes growled, standing.

"We have a translation. Potentially an inaccurate one, but I'm inclined to think otherwise," Amaia corrected.

Ever the linguist, ever making certain of the correct word. Dawes didn't care. "That was more than we had an hour ago. Now we can figure out what it is they want. Who they *are.*"

"With the information regarding the Dreamscape," Amaia began, "it's fairly clear that these people are sending a pointed message. They're…well, 'watch us stand' is an almost combative phrase, suggesting that they're going to 'stand', metaphorically speaking, with or without the permission of the Republic."

"They're dissidents," Dawes said, "what do you expect?"

"This is more than just being contrary." Amaia frowned. "Like you said, they have to *want* something. Something more than just exposing the Konsulars as users of their Dreamscape. We need to figure it out."

"How would you suggest we go about doing that"? Finding out what they wanted had been his idea and was exactly what was needed to find these people and put this case behind him, but as soon as he said the words, Dawes knew it wasn't going to be easy. Why couldn't he have had a nice, simple case of someone taking more food rations than they were appointed? Okay, that wasn't strictly K.C. territory, but it would have been a nice step into Decommissioning. Instead, he was watching Amaia, a Citizen with far too many variables in her Placing to make sense, and also, the only one who could help him. She put her hand on a book and Dawes sighed.

"We have to learn more of the language," Amaia said. "There must be a reason why these people chose Eloaech. In order to figure out why, we have to understand Eloaech and its people."

"More research." Dawes wanted to hit the wall, but this wasn't his office and he didn't have any nanites. "Of course."

"It's all we have. Unless your efforts into discovering where the Dreamscape was manufactured have come up with something? No? I didn't think so," Amaia pointed out. She picked up a book and handed it to Dawes.

He took it disdainfully. "I wasn't Placed as a linguist, if you'll remember," he grumbled, thumbing through the pages. "This isn't what I do."

"I wasn't Placed as a linguist, either," Amaia snapped in return.

And wasn't that just the problem, Dawes thought before turning his attention to the book. *How could someone who wasn't Placed in the field be so capable?*

Dawes returned to his flat feeling wearier than he had since he had chased that foolish thief across the Ground Level of Kyper three years ago. His shoulders sagged, despite lack of physical exertion, his feet dragged, and he had a scowl set into his brow—a good indication to everyone that he should be left well alone.

Six hours. That was how long he had been at Amaia's office, working with her to piece the language and its people, as she said, together. They had come up with a general rule for conjugating verbs (from the infinitive with the ending *-uen* to the first person singular *-e*, then second person singular *-u*, then third person singular *-a*, with *-n* added to all of those for the plural forms), a collection of vocabulary, and something about cases for nouns. And that was just what they had done before lunch.

Dawes hadn't understood one word in seven that Amaia had said and felt as though he were back in school before his Placement. Knowledge that didn't quite fit was being wrung through his head, forcing him to think in ways that were unfamiliar and uncomfortable. It was unproductive and if it weren't for the fact that he needed to understand this language in order to find these people, he would have given up long ago. He cursed again the fact that the Interfaces couldn't retain any data about the language. He fed them everything he and Amaia found, but when he referenced it later, it was gone. Every single time.

After lunch—a wonderful time when his brain could stop trying to think about words and their structure—he was given a lesson in how language and culture intertwined. Language, Amaia had claimed, was a choice by every person that used it. Whether or not a person was speaking to someone of similar status determined what words were used. In formal versus informal settings, in situations of anger, of passion, or even just asking a stranger a question on the streets determined what words were used. That was only on an individual level. On a cultural level, a language could signify solidarity within a group, a merging of two cultures into one of mutual understanding, whether a people saw the world in distinctive colours or hues of the same.

Common, the language of the Republic, Amaia had explained, was a unifying force that allowed the Republic to form and also smooth out any dissenting forces within other languages and cultures. Everyone spoke the same language and therefore referred to—and thought about—the world in the same manner. Individually, there might be variations, but understanding was mutual.

All the lecture had done was make Dawes' head spin and instilled in him a headache, due to the fact that he was trying to think about his own words and the things they revealed about him via subconscious communicators.

He sank onto his couch and tossed his jacket aside, not caring where it landed.

"Incoming message from Daleni Itar," the pleasant female voice said.

Dawes groaned and leaned his head back on the couch. He didn't want to talk with Daleni Itar. He wanted a drink and a long sonic-shower.

"Answer. Hello, Citizen," Dawes rasped.

"Citizen. Maddox," Daleni Itar's image appeared on the display wall, though Dawes made no effort to lift his head. "I've received a very interesting note from a Salesh Ramani regarding you."

"Who"?

"A Konsular who says that he spoke with you yesterday evening. In fact, he says that he was dragged out of bed to one of our labs in order to talk with you," Daleni Itar sounded particularly irked. Dawes sighed. So *that* was the Konsular's name. He had never been introduced and had, obviously foolishly, assumed that the two of them would never cross paths and the issue wouldn't come up again.

"Did he say why he was 'dragged' to the lab? Because I needed information on an analysis of the Dreamscape the victims of my attacks were doped with," Dawes grumbled.

"He explained," Daleni Itar's frown could be heard in her voice, enough so that Dawes lifted his head and stared openly at her. She looked tired. More so than he had ever seen before. Those two words said everything and yet there was something more. An implied meaning.

"And"? Dawes sat up, mind already working to break down her tone, intonation, facial expressions, words. He caught himself a moment later. *I'm not the linguist. Amaia would know better than I about this.* Dawes flicked his fingers and started recording the call for later examination.

"If I make one mention of the matter, my career is at an end, Placement or not. Konsulars have no tolerance for weakness and failure, no matter I've done my duty. I'm going to ask you again, Maddox, what have you learned? We need to catch these people and get them off the streets. The order of the Republic is at stake." The head of K.C. narrowed her eyes and practically bared her teeth at Dawes, enough so that he felt the weight of his position in relation to hers. His Placement was not nearly as highly-ranked and yet here she was, demanding his help. Just as he had demanded the same of Amaia.

"The language is the important piece," Dawes said. "Coupled with the Dreamscape, it's a pointed attack. So deciphering the language and why that particular one was chosen is important."

"Why"?

"Because a secret language—one used to communicate out of sight of the authorities—reveals a lot about the mindset of the group. Eloaech, the language these people are using, is meant to have been used by an ancient, pre-Republic group of wanderers. These wanderers valued..." Dawes tried to recall the exact wording that Amaia had given him and snapped his fingers as the phrase came to mind "... knowledge, but more, the variety of knowledge that a variety of experiences can give. They valued a person's freedom and right to choose a life path above all else, because it gave that person a unique perspective and thereby granted unique knowledge, the compilation of which was their purpose."

"So, what, these people are a bunch of knowledge seekers?" Daleni Itar scoffed. Dawes shrugged.

"Amaia, the linguist, and I haven't figured out quite what those values have to do with these people. At the moment, all we know for certain is that the message—whatever it is—is pointed directly at the Konsulars and Tech-Elite, the cornerstones of the Republic as we know it."

Daleni Itar pinched the bridge of her nose and closed her eyes. "That's all"?

"That's more than we had yesterday. We are so close to figuring out who these people are, what they want. We need a little more time," Dawes said.

"What about the Dreamscape? Did the lab tell you nothing?" Daleni Itar's voice was cold, a much worse fate than the fiery anger that she often displayed. That alone told Dawes that things weren't going well. He rubbed his jaw with the heel of his palm.

"They only told me that the Dreamscape used in the bash-and-dashes was the same as that the Konsulars and CoreTech elite use. The Konsular didn't tell me how he procured the drug, if he even knows. And none of my investigations have told me anything. All we know is that it's the same. And it's made by the dissidents."

"I suggest you find out where this Dreamscape is coming from," Daleni Itar said slowly, her lip curling.

"Short of demanding an interview with the Konsular to discover how he obtains his drugs, I don't think that's going to—"

"Fool," Daleni Itar hissed. Dawes tightened his jaw and looked away from the holographic projection. If only to keep her from seeing the anger in his eyes, he thought. But let her take it as a sign of submission. He only wanted his Decomissioning. "Don't you think that if the Konsular had *known* such a thing, he would have told you"?

Dawes mumbled something, but she had a point. To have to admit the Dreamscape usage at all must have been…humiliating? Weak? Dawes didn't know the right word. He would bet good, illegal nanites, though, that Amia would. In any case, the only thing worse to a Konsular than admitting weakness to a lower Placement were dissidents. Dreamscape use affected one Konsular and a handful of Citizens. Dissdents affected the entire Republic.

Dawes clenched his fists and lifted his eyes. "I need more time."

"Fine," Daleni Itar said flatly, her weariness plain. "But only because I have no other course available to me. The more time you take, the more time these people have to work. Their attacks are becoming dangerous to morale, Maddox. People are afraid to go out after dark. Military Intelligence is talking about having us enforce a curfew, to keep potential drug dealers off the streets, just in case these dissidents are selling to the average Placements. You keep working. You and that linguist of yours. Am I clear?"

"Perfectly. Goodbye, Citizen," Dawes said. If he didn't find out who was behind this and what they wanted soon, everything that happened to upset the balance of the Republic was going to be on his head. Daleni Itar would make sure of that.

He was beginning to find the meaning behind a person's choice of words as a bit amazing.

9

Salesh Ramani made certain his door was locked before he sat down at his table. He had ordered a special dinner from the cooks who were Placed at Konsular beck and call. He was glad he hadn't been Placed as a cook or a delivery person, speeder mechanic, anything else. Konsular suited him perfectly well, and not just for the good food.

The situation that made Ramani lock his door, when on principle he never bothered, was the small syringe sitting next to his steaming food. Dreamscape. It made his problems easier to bear and smoothed out situations that would otherwise have him itching in discomfort. Dealing with people outside of Konsular status, having to handle the minor political situations that wracked the Republic, and the covering up of those situations. Not even a supposedly-united world was without its problems, and the various regions of the Republic were notorious for demanding resources or concessions. The average person didn't care, certainly, as they were Placed where they needed to be and never moved outside of their purview. But other Konsulars and the ambitions of the Tech-Elite…

Ramani injected the syringe into his arm, and a few moments later, his problems simply melted away. He could enjoy the smells of his food before him, each taste of the meal on his fork so much stronger than anyone else could possibly imagine. He swallowed with a sigh of pleasure and sank into his cushioned chair, thinking about the events of the day. His thoughts were free from any stress the day had brought.

That Inspector sprang foremost to his mind. Dogged. He might even be the one to catch the dissidents. Who would want to dissent against the Republic? Things were working out so well. Trade within the Republic was increasing, the Tech-Elite were pushing their Interfaces for progress and trade with the Outer Planets which was starting to really take hold. There were squabbles among Konsulars, sure, but he had everything he needed. Wanted. Could Possibly Imagine.

"Hello, Konsular," a voice broke into Ramani's thoughts and he smiled at the intrusion. He should have felt frightened, even angry, but now he had company and that was important. It didn't matter that the company had managed to break through his locks or that this person had forgone the official greeting, twisting it to evoke his title and power. The person was impossible to identify, wearing all black clothing with a fine, black mesh over the face to hide identity and a distorter to hide their voice. Male or female, strong or weak, dark-skinned or the pale that indicated Wasteland heritage, he didn't know. And it didn't matter.

Ramani frowned, trying to force logical thought through those feelings. It *should* matter. Dreamscape made his positive emotions stronger and blocked out the negative, but it never made him as unreasonable as this. "Something is off." He smiled at his guest, who nodded.

"That's correct, Konsular," the person said. "Your dosage was increased rather a lot. I imagine that you'll be a bit jaded tomorrow, but a little cynicism can be healthy in a person."

"Who are you?" Ramani asked. He reached for his fork to take another bite of food and paused, thinking that it might be rude. "Would you care for something to eat"?

"I thank you, but no." The figure sat across the table from Ramani and propped head in hand. "As to who I am, I believe that you already know the answer to that question."

"The dissidents," Ramani said and, to his mild surprise, quiet admiration—a result of the Dreamscape—began to form in his mind. Interesting effect, he thought, as Dreamscape had never changed his opinion of something, merely made it less annoying to deal with. Perhaps the higher dose attributed to that.

"Yes," the figure said. "They are mine. As you soon will be."

No anger at the statement, just interest. Ramani leaned back in his chair and decided that having a drink of his wine would do no harm. He drank, the flavours hitting his tongue sharply, making him wonder whether he had ever tasted wine so good.

"I see you do not comprehend," the person said, nodding. "You don't understand why I am doing this. But you will, once you answer a few questions for me."

"Very well," Ramani smiled pleasantly.

"Who prepared your food"?

Was that a hint of a sneer in the voice of his guest? Ramani couldn't tell, nor did he care. "Cooks. And it was delivered by the Delivery service. Just as every meal is, for everyone in the Republic." Ramani took another sip of his wine and licked a few drops off his lips, amazed at the intensity.

"And who cleans your flat"?

"These are unusual questions." Ramani chuckled. "The Cleaners, of course. For me, as for everyone in the Republic. Though, I admit, my flat is considerably nicer than most people, on account of my status as a Konsular. Konsulars are second only to the Head of the Republic. We get the best."

"Naturally. One so obviously capable as you, tested by both aptitude and genetics to be Placed as Konsular, how could you possibly deserve anything less." This time, there was no mistaking the scorn in the figure's voice and Ramani found himself frowning, though it was difficult and muddied his thoughts.

"I don't—"

"Understand? Of course not," the figure said. "I was just making a point."

"What point is that? That everything in the Republic is ordered perfectly; that people are Placed exactly where they need to be? Specialisation of the people is nothing to sneer at, my friend. It has taken many years and the help of the Interface for the Republic to become so efficient. People are Placed where they function best," Ramani said.

"Yes, and they do exactly as they are told in order to complete their duty for the Republic. There is no choice in the matter." The last words were spoken with a hiss, and for the first time since the intruder entered, Ramani felt a stab of fear break through the Dreamscape. The high dose was wearing off. He was beginning to understand one thing: he was in danger.

"Choice"? Ramani laughed nervously, trying to maintain the semblance of pleasure that the Dreamscape provided. The figure's head tilted to one side a mere fraction of an inch, but it was enough to make Ramani sweat. "What does choice have to do with anything? The people are Placed exactly where it suits them. Nothing outside of their capabilities is asked; they are provided with every need as accorded their status and—"

"And you never once ask them what they want," the figure growled, the distorter making the sound harsh. Ramani swallowed a wince and thanked the Republic that he was a Konsular and used to dealing with difficult people. Though never a dissident.

"They are happy—"

"Because they know no better. These people are not individuals, part of a greater good. They are drones, unable to think for themselves, unable to innovate or question or choose to be something other than what the Republic tells them. And it's killing them. *That's* what I fight for, Salesh," the figure was oddly calm for the intensity of the words. That, more than the fact that his locks had been broken and he couldn't quite shake off the Dreamscape enough to muster the will to summon help, scared Ramani.

"Are you here to kill me"? He licked his lips, as he had done but minutes before, only this time there was no wine, no ecstasy. Only the bile in his throat that stung of fear.

"Kill you"? The figure tossed back its head and laughed, the sound alien and harsh. "No, my dear Konsular Ramani. I am here to offer you the opportunity to find out what choice feels like."

"This doesn't feel like choice," Ramani spat, a false front of strength. It was futile, he knew, as his hands were shaking tremendously, both from coming off the initial high of Dreamscape and pure terror-fuelled adrenaline.

"I haven't offered it to you, yet," the figure said, and if it weren't for the fact that Ramani couldn't see the face of the intruder, he would have sworn the dissident smiled. "It has recently come to my attention—via recorded communications and lab reports, all cleverly smuggled through Privacy Control—that the Konsulars and the Tech-Elite are issued Dreamscape in order to make their dealings with the rest of the less-enlightened population more…bearable. I have known this for some time, hence the use of Dreamscape, particularly *your* Dreamscape, in my motions on your speeders. These lab reports." The figure waved a wrist and the holoscreens on Ramani's walls lit to life, something that should have been impossible with biometric printing. Impossible didn't seem to matter to this person. Ramani swallowed nervously as he saw the reports from the lab analysis of the Dreamscape, which clearly linked it to the Konsular and Tech-Elite.

"Yes, I see you are aware of my reach," the figure said. "These reports were confirmation that *you* were aware of my knowledge of your use of Dreamscape. *My* Dreamscape, incidentally. That lets me offer you a choice."

"I still see no choice," Ramani tore his gaze away from the holoscreens and faced the figure. The initial high was wearing off, but the longer effects were still very much in place, and he found that he could do nothing more than feel fear and its adrenaline, both of which were fading as he grasped at the pleasure of not being killed.

"Here is the choice, then," the figure's voice was no longer playful, even amused, but flat, perfectly, deadly serious. "Either you say absolutely nothing about my visit, my purposes, and promise to inform me of any further developments in this investigation, or I release these lab reports across every screen in the Republic. Your name will, of course, be prominently mentioned. The Republic will blame you for the spread of Dreamscape and there will be a great deal of mistrust for rather a long time. Your petty political squabbles with other Konsulars will mean nothing in comparison to the chaos one little slip of the privacy screen will cause."

Ramani's jaw fell slack and he struggled against the Dreamscape to try and find a means out of the situation. He was one of the top-ranked Konsulars. In a few years, he could be on the way to the office of the Head of the Republic. He could manoeuvre his way through fraught situations. And one "nobody" with a few computer skills had him backed into a corner.

"This is no choice. Keep quiet and help you or every problem in the Republic will fall on my shoulders," Ramani hissed. The figure shrugged one shoulder.

"It is a choice. Just because it isn't a good one doesn't mean that the ability to choose isn't there."

"You are going to get caught and you will rot in the highest-security Republic prison for the rest of your life," Ramani tried to shout, but his voice wouldn't cooperate. All he managed was a rasp.

"Perhaps. But not right now. Right now, you have a choice to make. And I feel as though I have already been patient enough. Ten seconds, Konsular." The no-nonsense tone was back and Ramani shuddered, torn between positive emotions and pain. He wet his mouth with wine and once more tasted more than he ever had before. He closed his eyes, feeling sweat trickle down his brow. He had never had to choose something like this before. It *hurt* and yet the Dreamscape made it better. Made it alright. He wanted to run and remain, simultaneously, and his thoughts were also being pulled in different directions.

"Very well," Ramani breathed, pressing the heels of his palms to his eyes to regain equilibrium. "I will inform you of anything regarding the investigation. And I will keep quiet about this visit and your purposes for coming."

"Good choice," the figure said. When Ramani lowered his hands, the figure was gone, no formal farewell to signify that the person had gone. In the figure's place, fairly gleaming in the light of Ramani's flat was another syringe. Without hesitation, Ramani leaned forwards to grab it and plunged the needle into his arm. The pain of his encounter melted away completely and Ramani sighed, settling back in his chair. Now he could think clearly. But the food was on the table, and he no longer cared that his wine was half-gone and the food was no longer warm. He refilled his glass and settled down to eat, each bite flavourful, like nothing he had ever before tasted.

10

"**I** found something to call them," Dawes said, his head resting on his hand as he flipped absently through the pages of a book. As eager as he was to figure out what the language meant to these people, researching the language was, to him, another matter entirely.

Amaia looked up from where she was transcribing scraps of Eloaech onto the board. "Oh? Something other than a bunch of cowardly dissidents who couldn't have waited until *after* your Decommissioning to stir up trouble?" Amaia turned back to her board and underlined a phrase before grumbling under her breath.

"Yes," Dawes shoved one of the older scraps of paper towards her.

She sighed and leaned over the table, looking at the paper. "Ske'toa," she said, her voice giving a slight break in the middle of the word, something Dawes had learned was called a glottal stop. He couldn't replicate it to save his life. "One of the compounded titular words, this one meaning…really? Malevolent spirit?"

"It seemed to fit." Dawes pushed away from the table to stand and pace over to the windows. Looking out on the University campus, where subject-experts were walking swiftly from one class to another, each neatly labelled by the coloured uniform they wore. Biologists in lavender, Chemists in ochre, Journalists in yellow. It was all so neat, everyone belonged somewhere. No dissent, no suggestion that these people could be targeting the Republic.

"Ske'toa is a singular term, meant only to apply to one person," Amaia said. She paused, waiting for his response. Dawes was too tired to reply. He felt like Daleni Itar had looked the other day: weary. This whole thing was weighing on his mind and he didn't know how to stop it. "We can call their leader Ske'toa, if that helps. The others can still be dissidents."

"Fine," Dawes rubbed his forehead and felt, not for the first time, wrinkles there. He was old, relatively speaking. What was he doing seeking out battles with a group of rebels eager for a fight?

"Well, I like it," Amaia nodded firmly. She paused again and sighed. "Alright, what's wrong"?

"What do you mean?" Dawes snarled, two shades darker than his usual growls.

"You're not as invested in this research as you usually are. Not to mention you're taking my head off for agreeing with you about Ske'toa," Amaia said. "Now you're standing here by the window, brooding."

"I am not brooding," Dawes said.

"Alright, what word would you choose to describe the soulful, slightly sulking stare at the University campus?" Amaia asked, folding her arms.

Dawes sighed and shrugged.

That was the problem. The words. He had started researching and being instructed in a subject that wasn't anywhere near what he normally did. It was foreign to him and yet the methods of thinking about things were similar. Break a problem down into its component pieces and analyse each individually. Then put them together and see what it meant as a whole, in context. Then you could see what it meant and do something about it. Only, thinking about words, about the different words he chose in different situations, about how a sentence sounded if he used one word versus another, how meaning changed with a difference in intonation and stress—a phrase could become a question, an object could take on more meaning—it was enough to make his head spin.

He hadn't realised how much unconscious thought went into language. It was one more burden on his mind now that he had been introduced to the significance. It was unfamiliar. Taxing. And it didn't seem to get him anywhere with his current case.

"This is…out of my area of expertise. I am used to compiling data gathered by myself and the Interfaces and seeing which suspect matches the data. I then find the person or persons, chase them if need be, arrest them, and that's that." Dawes hunched his shoulders, staring out at the University, he saw nothing but his own thoughts. "This?" he laughed drily, "this is not what I'm capable of."

"You seem perfectly capable to me," Amaia smiled cheekily, nudging his arm.

"Well, I'm not," Dawes snapped, inching away from her. "Do you want to know why? Because I'm not made for it. I was Placed as an agent of Kyper Central, not a researcher, not a linguist, not a Konsular. I have one set of skills and that is all. This whole exercise is nothing more than a charade. I will fail, undoubtedly, and be sent off to Rabesh to live out my Decommissioning. I will die years before my time. Daleni Itar, my superior and the head of K.C., will be deemed incapable of maintaining control of her underlings and will fall. The Konsulars will come in and soothe away public worry, all the while, these…these… rebels—there, I've said it—are only going to gain a foothold."

"By your reasoning, then," Amaia cut in, her voice mocking, her eyes flashing, "the Republic is going to fall to chaos and rebellion because *you* were Placed at Kyper Central?"

"Yes," Dawes growled.

"That's a load of *garai*," Amaia plucked an Eloaech term from the air, and while Dawes didn't know what it meant, he had a fair idea. "A person is capable of far more than what some computer Interface says based on genetic testing and aptitude tests taken as a child while the brain is still developing."

"Oh, really. And you know better than a system that has worked for three generations? Which eliminates unemployment and gives everyone a purpose, providing people with partners who are similar in physique, thought process, ability, all provided according to need and capability?"

"I know that I wasn't Placed as a linguist," Amaia raised her chin enough for pride. "I wasn't Placed anywhere specific. I *chose* what I wanted to do with my life. Now look at me. I'm an expert in a Republic that didn't have a place built for me. I've learned things that might not have come easily to me. I've had to learn about vast amounts of material that has nothing to do with language because I needed to understand people. History. Physics. Economics. I saw that as necessary for what I needed to learn and so I learned it."

"You were Placed as a subject-specialist, though," Dawes pointed out. "I'm just—"

"An Inspector. You said it yourself, you gathered data and analysed it. That's all that I do. So, gather data. Analyse it. Stop feeling sorry for yourself because these rebels are making you work a bit." Amaia turned on her heel and stalked over to the board scrawled with writing. She glared at it, her hands folded across her chest, her lips moving as she mumbled over the words.

Silence filled the room, and with it, a tension that was almost palpable. Dawes felt the weight of her words as much as he felt the truth of them. Still, he was tired and wanted nothing more than to give up. Surely there was someone in the Republic more qualified, better Placed for this sort of situation. Military Intelligence, though their views were directed towards potential attacks from other sources—mass terrorists, outworlders and the like—could help. So far, the situation was restricted to Kyper, which meant that they would only step in when things began to fail catastrophically.

That left only himself and Amaia—who was willing to assist, despite the fact that investigation wasn't her Placement. Maybe she was right. He had been taught when first assigned to K.C. He had lessons and work and had made more than a few mistakes. Placement had put him there, but he had worked to stay where he was.

"You may be right," Dawes said, his voice soft, yet echoing through the room.

"Rethink your words," Amaia said, though her growl was playful rather than hurt. "I *am* right."

"You're very young to be so sure of yourself," Dawes retorted.

"And you're quite old to be so doubtful." Amaia turned and fisted her hands on her hips. "Alright, Inspector, what's next"?

"A good deal of reexamination," Dawes decided, turning back towards the room. When he had first arrived, it was ordered, each book in its place and the table relatively clear. Now there were papers scattered over every available surface, with at least three notebooks ready to be written in, not to mention the mess that was on the board. There were books stacked on the floor, taken from the Archives at the University—a place where few people had ventured for many years—and remnants of meals the Cleaners had yet to clear away. The chaos, though, lent itself to a sort of pride.

Dawes sat in his chair and stretched. "We need to know what these people want. We know who they're talking to, we know what language they're using, we even know what it is they're saying. We don't know why, though."

"Well, before you interrupted with your titbit about Ske'toa," Amaia sat at the table across from him and pushed her notebook towards him, "I was going to say that I had found something of interest."

"*Chi kai e Eloai. Chi kaieno shraija e Eloai. Chi kaiesh shraija e Eloai.* Something about a wanderer has something and is something. The first one is 'a wanderer is'…something, right? Because there's no form of to be in the present tense?" Dawes closed his eyes to remember the details, the information coming to mind after a few moments thought. When he opened his eyes and saw Amaia nodding, he grinned. There was a stab of pain, too, as he recalled that he had thought to be incapable of doing such things. Self-doubt hurt.

"Right. The verb *shraija* is the third person singular of 'to have'. *Chi kai* and its variants are the important piece, though. I think this is meant to be a statement of the basic tenets of the philosophy of the wanderers. *Chi kai* is free. *Chi kaieno* is freedom of thought and *chi kaiesh* freedom of action. A wanderer is free. A wanderer has freedom of thought. A wanderer has freedom of action." Amaia's voice was quiet as she looked down at the pages in her hand.

Her eyes flicked up to meet Dawes', though her head did not move. It was a full three seconds before he realised what she had found, what the words meant. "By the Republic. These dissidents are trying to tear down all instances of the Republic telling them what to do."

"And the Konsulars, according to Ske'toa, are the ones to blame," Amaia breathed.

"Not just that, but the entire system upon which the Republic is built. You said it yourself: people are Placed. A position is chosen for a citizen, not the other way around. The entire social stratus of the Republic is based on Placement, including ration availability, housing, social interaction, everything."

"I'm not sure I understand," Amaia said. The look in her eyes said plainly that she did. Perhaps she could not stomach saying it out loud. Dawes was having a hard enough time; the words seemed to choke in his throat and all that was left was the recourse of his body. But he had to speak. He had to say the words.

"These people have already shown an ability to bypass Republic security and privacy measures. The attacks on the speeders, the messages across the screens, those were just to get our attention," Dawes said. "If they intend to attack, not just talk, things are going to get a whole lot worse."

11

Salesh Ramani scratched the back of his hand absently, staring at the group of children gathered before him with glazed-over eyes. He knew that his presence there was an integral part of the process by which they were to learn their Places within the Republic, and also that if he did this, his own place would advance, but these children were so…undeveloped. They hadn't been Placed, they weren't the progeny of any politicians or high-level workers, that he knew of, and they watched him hungrily. He held the power, the blood that would open the testing platform and allow them to be Placed. The children knew that and Ramani knew that. He stifled a yawn.

"Today is a great day," the teacher said. She was a teacher of the undetermined, Placed so that she could impart knowledge about the Republic and the duties that each person held to the great system that allowed everyone to work and live in comfort and peace. She didn't communicate directly with Ramani. "Today you are going to take the second test that will Place you into your proper quarters within the Republic. At birth, you were tested, now those and these results will be concatenated by the Interfaces so that you may become what you were meant to be. Now, you are going to become Citizens."

Ramani cleared his throat, somewhat impatient to get on with the procedure. He had other duties to perform.

The teacher straightened her posture.

"This man," she gestured to him, "is going to unlock the platform and you will each step into the chamber where you will be tested. Each and every one of you has a place in the Republic. The Republic provides. The Republic cares. Without you, the Republic would not move forward."

It wasn't a motto that Ramani recognised, but this was a quiet sector of Kyper and that could easily mean the motto had been modified. These were the progeny of the cooks and mechanics and factory workers of the sector and the Republic had to ensure their dedication. Everything worked smoothly in the Republic, or it didn't work at all. That was the motto *he* knew. The one *he* lived by. Similar, but different.

Ramani stepped forwards after the children had finished parroting the motto and pressed his hand against the sensor. He was pricked and a drop of his blood extracted. The platform hummed to life and the chamber doors opened. "Welcome to the Placement test," a pleasant female voice intoned. The teacher nodded her head eagerly and pushed the first child—a young boy wearing the deep blue factory uniform of the district—forwards.

This was the part that Ramani hated. The child would enter, the test would take about ten minutes and then the child would emerge, a large smile as the computer spoke the child's Placement. It was a long process and he had to stand there, congratulating each and every child. Direct interaction. He was one of the younger Konsulars, so this odious job fell to him.

He pushed his hands into the pockets on his tunic that hung at ribcage-level. The fabric was fine and a calming shade of grey, an indication of his position. Inside the right-hand pocket was a vial, inside the left, a syringe. They comforted him.

The boy stepped up to the platform and then something unexpected happened. Instead of waiting until the boy was inside, the doors slammed shut and the platform powered down.

Ramani widened his eyes in the most overt display of emotion he had shown to ordinary Citizens for many years.

"My dear Citizens. Instead of forcing the boy into a Place," a voice rang out in the computer's stead. It was distorted enough that it did not sound male nor female, merely powerful, "try letting him choose. *Nehrun tai hanen! Chi kai e Eloai!*"

The lights in the room went dark and moments later the other children began to whimper in fear. Ramani cleared his throat, "Lights."

Nothing happened. No hum from the computer, no response from the Interface, not even a buzz of denial. Just the whimpering of children and those words still echoing through the air. Or perhaps they weren't echoing in the air but through Ramani's head. The voice he knew, intimately, the words by report from Inspector Dawes. He tightened his hand around the vial in his pocket and nearly drew out the Dreamscape then and there. The dissident, what Inspector Dawes and his pet linguist had taken to calling Ske'toa, instilled enough fear in Ramani to need the Dreamscape. He had to wipe out that fear, had to bring pleasure to escape from pain.

The Konsular closed his eyes and swallowed, trying to force down the desire for Dreamscape long enough to let him think. He couldn't dose himself just then. There was the teacher and the children to consider. Should any one of them see him dose himself and then speak on it, or worse, make a report of it, he would be in serious trouble. A breach of that kind would mean the end of his title of Konsular.

He would become nothing more than a low-level government official, a Bureaucrat, unable to leave the buildings. He would still have his Dreamscape, but it would be looked down upon rather than accepted. He would have to huddle in back alleys to buy the drug from people who had no business having it. People who were owned by Ske'toa.

It was bad enough he had to report to that fell person. Every evening, a message that never appeared on any of the official servers, waited. Demanding updates. The information was thin enough that Ramani was always trembling by the time he entered it in. Would this Ske'toa think he wasn't telling everything? Would the incompetence of Kyper Central mean the end of his life in the Republic? He sent the messages, and ten minutes later, a courier appeared at his door with a vial of Dreamscape.

Ramani swallowed again and withdrew his hand from his pocket, shaking as he did so. He thanked the Republic that the lights were still out, and the computer didn't seem to be functioning. Had anyone seen…

"Konsular," the teacher spoke in a hushed voice, obviously afraid. "Shouldn't they have sent help by now"?

"Kyper Central will deal with the situation," Ramani said firmly. "They have likely already dispatched a speeder with an Interface technician to remedy the situation."

"Thank the Republic," the teacher said. She was nothing more than a silhouette in the darkened room, the lights seeping in from a crack in the door. As it was automated, Ramani knew that it wouldn't open. Ske'toa had done the job well, no matter that it was deplorable. A morsel of respect took hold in Ramani and, no matter how he tried, he could not dislodge it. It was as permanent as the desire for Dreamscape. It could be pushed aside for a moment, but eventually, he would give in.

"Children, Kyper Central has sent someone to help and they should be here soon," the teacher soothed her charges, who moved towards her in the dim light. "Surely it is nothing more than a malfunction in the computer matrix of the building. Nothing to fret about."

"Will our Placement happen now? The voice said that we had to choose what we—"

"That was nothing more than a computer virus," the teacher scolded the young girl who spoke. "Your Placement will be rescheduled once a suitable building has been found while this one is being repaired."

For a brief moment, Ramani wished that his worries could be soothed as easily as the teacher soothed her students. She had been Placed as a teacher and so had a talent for dealing with the worries of children, but even so, there was something inherently calming in her voice. A safe haven in a storm where nothing but wind and rain should exist. The moment was short, though, as Ramani recalled the voice—Ske'toa—that had spoken. He doubted very much that there was a speeder from K.C. on the way. He also doubted that these children would be Placed any time soon. They had been marked by Ske'toa merely because he was present, but now they would be kept from Placement as a reminder. A message. This message, though, was not just for Konsular Salesh Ramani and those investigators at Kyper Central. It was for all of the Republic.

The children would tell their parents, who would tell their neighbours, who would tell their co-workers. If it weren't for the fact that the children were the offspring of factory workers and cooks, Ramani imagined that the news would spread across the city like wildfire. As it was, the news would remain in the communes of the maintenance workers and factory hands for a day or two before spreading across the city. Was the delay a good thing or a bad? Was it enough to do damage control or would the delay make things worse? It was a question for the Public Relations department, but Ramani couldn't help asking. His input would be crucial and yet there was one thing he would never be able to tell them.

"Konsular?" the teacher asked after a few minutes. "How long will the speeder be"?

"I don't know," Ramani said. "But I would suggest making yourselves comfortable. To, ah, find an Interface worker could take time. They are very valuable, and their time cannot be taken away from crucially important tasks." Lies. Each word he plucked from the air was a carefully constructed lie, one founded on the importance of his Placement. Of course, he would know; of course, he would have the answers, else why would he be Placed in such an important position.

Ramani pushed his thoughts away from such a line of inquiry. If he started thinking about such things, about the lies he was able to tell, about the fact that he could demand just about anything from anyone in the name of public morale and duty to the Republic, if he looked too closely, he would be in severe danger of examining himself. Discovering just what sort of person he was and putting his feelings above the good of the Republic. The Republic came first, not his questions about what it took to keep the Republic going. Just because the average Citizens didn't know what the Konsulars had to do to keep the Republic working smoothly didn't mean that the Konsulars weren't working for the good of everyone.

Such obedience as his Placement and ability allowed was much easier with Dreamscape to dull the edges. It made it so much easier not to feel the contempt and mild pity for those who were shuffled into place for the good of all. Made it so much easier to sign orders and issue directives that let the distribution of services be tightly controlled, promising more if people did their duty to the Republic, if they obeyed without question. Because what were questions but hindrances to duty?

Ske'toa's words came to Ramani, though he tried to push them away. Choice. Freedom. *For what purpose?* What would giving people the ability to choose what they wanted out of life accomplish? The Republic would lose out on the advantage of having people exactly where they were needed. The people would have to provide for themselves, not live securely in the knowledge that the Republic would provide for them. They would have to live with inequality, with the knowledge that some were willing to work harder and had better ideas and would invariably do better in life than others, versus the fact that everyone was equal in the Republic. The need of the state was all that mattered—the Konsulars had more strain due to their work, so they required more; the factory workers could allow their minds to relax while their bodies eased into the rhythm of work, so they required less. All their needs were provided for, everyone was equally happy under the Republic. Their goals were for the common good, not individual interest.

Choice. Freedom.

Ramani pressed his hands to his eyes, gritting his teeth, glad of the dark so no one else would see what he was doing. His struggle was a secret sort of shame that he would not allow anyone else to see. He had never questioned anything about the Republic before; he was not doing so now. As long as he didn't look too hard, didn't think too hard, there was no need to even consider the ridiculous nature of Ske'toa's words.

Who was Ske'toa, anyways? Some sort of dissident, or worse, a rebel, who had never been able to obey, who never thought about anything but himself—herself? The secrecy grated on Ramani—and ignored the common good completely. Why should Ramani pay any heed to such a creature? Ske'toa obviously didn't understand anything about how society worked. Ramani did. He understood how things worked, why duty to the Republic mattered above all else.

While it was still dark, while he could still hold onto that feeling of pleasure at being in possession of knowledge others did not have, Ramani reached into his pockets and quickly filled the syringe, tapping it twice to remove air bubbles, then plunged the needle into his arm. He felt his muscles relax, and that feeling of pride swelled. He slipped his Dreamscape back into his pocket and waited, tuning out the quiet drone of the children's talk and the older tones of the teacher.

He didn't know how long they waited for the speeder, nor did he care. The Dreamscape kept his emotions in check, and he was as unconcerned with the others in the room as he was with the weather near Crepuscule, that is to say, not at all. Ramani merely saw that the light in the room shifted and the power returned, leaving a concerned looking woman in K.C. uniform and an Interface maintenance worker. Ramani stood and, without a word, brushed past the teacher and children to stand before the K.C. woman.

"Send for Inspector Dawes," Ramani said, ignoring formality in his haze. His voice sounded cool and crisp to his own ears, but he felt no more than a flicker of annoyance, as if an insect were flying around his head. "And that fool woman he seems to be so attached to. She'll know sooner or later, anyways."

"Of course, Konsular." The woman lifted her sleeve to her mouth and spoke into the transmitter that relayed her signal back to Kyper Central. In a matter of minutes, Dawes and Amaia were ushered into the now-empty room where the Placements were to be held. If either seemed surprised to find Ramani staring with distaste-softened-by-curiosity at the computer chamber, neither showed it. Nor did they react when he turned to them and they saw the dilated pupils, the drug-induced calm. Any other people would have just believed that it was merely the calm of a Konsular, the reason for his Placement into the position.

Both knew otherwise. Both kept silent.

Ramani straightened his stance and stared at them with all the calm he possessed. "I thought you were getting a handle on this person. This Ske'toa and the other dissidents."

"As far as we can tell, it's just the one person doing the attacks," Dawes said. "And Ske'toa is far more capable at breaking into the Interface than we had expected."

"Have you *any* idea where this person is? Who this person is?" Ramani looked back at the computer chamber and gave a quick shudder that not even Dreamscape could hide.

"We know what Ske'toa wants," Amaia spoke, her voice nowhere near as demure as Ramani would have expected. Did she know who he was? Or was her involvement in this investigation giving her ideas outside of her realm of expertise. "Ske'toa wants freedom of both thought and action. Wants people to be able to choose their life. Which is probably why this was the first open target, the first where everyone involved was able to understand the message."

"And stopping the speeders in Kyper for a full fifteen minutes while that stupid message played across the screen wasn't open? Taking down the Interface to have the city come to a standstill while another one of those messages played, that wasn't open?" The Dreamscape was wearing off. Ramani could feel his anger burning through the drug, making it harder work to calm his negative emotions. He wanted another fix, was inches away from needing another fix, but he couldn't give in. These two knew his secret, his weakness, and if there was anything he disliked more than feeling the full force of his uncontrolled emotions, it was appearing as weak.

"That was to get our attention," Amaia replied, growing bolder, making Ramani grind his teeth together. "No one understood what was going on because no one understood the message. It wasn't a statement, it was a means of creating uncertainty and fear. A different form of communication, with a slightly different result. It's similar to how people say one thing and an entirely different message comes across. You were understanding one level—or you did, once we deciphered the words—and the rest were understanding a different level. This message, pointedly stopping a Placement and saying, with no chance of misunderstanding, of what was meant, was the first open statement. Everyone understood. And that means Ske'toa is no longer looking just to you for acknowledgement, but to—"

"Acknowledgement"? Ramani curled his lip to hide his confusion. "Why would acknowledgement matter"?

"Without acknowledgement, there is no transmission of the message," Amaia waved her hand as if it were obvious, and Ramani found himself in the unusual position of understanding, and even admiring, but also disliking. "Ske'toa has gotten your attention, and now everyone is going to see what Ske'toa wants. Everyone is going to hear the message."

"But it doesn't make sense," Ramani snarled, rounding on Dawes. At least the Inspector was someone that Ramani could dislike without admiration. "The Placement will be rescheduled, and the children believe it was just a malfunction. Nothing lasting happened!"

"Are you sure?" Dawes asked quietly. "The thought has entered their head that they might choose their path rather than having it chosen for them. They might not accept it, but children are pliable. That's why they're Placed at such a young age, isn't it? To mould them into their Placement."

Ramani knew the Dreamscape was completely gone at this point. There was too much roiling anger and disgust and, yes, fear pounding its way through his veins to have been tamed by the drug. He was running on uncontrolled emotion and that thought terrified him nearly as much as the words of Dawes. "That is stepping very close to rebellious thoughts, Inspector. I suggest you reexamine your premises."

"It was only a thought," Dawes bowed his head in acknowledgement of Ramani's position, but the Konsular would have sworn he saw a flash of enlightenment in the Inspector's eyes. The meeting he had endured with Ske'toa only a short few days before came to mind and Ramani shuddered, shoving his hands into his pockets. Something in the calm, almost mocking voice of Ske'toa, his keeper and greatest enemy, reminded him of the Inspector. And then there was that woman, Amaia, who just watched as if she saw and understood everything. She was only a linguist, though. This, whatever it was, lay far outside her realm. But then, she was obviously involved in this investigation as more than a linguist. It appeared that she, too, was overstepping her bounds.

Ramani lifted his head and stalked out of the room without so much as a by-your-leave, silently demanding that they figure things out. He appropriated one of the K.C. speeders to take him to his office and only allowed himself to think when he was safely ensconced in the metal and glass of the speeder. His thought: did they know?

12

"We that loved him so, followed him, honored him
Lived in his mild and magnificent eye
Learned his great language, caught his clear accents
Made him our pattern to live and to die!"
—R. Browning, *The Last Leader*

A dark-skinned girl slipped through the shadows and knocked twice on the door of one of the tall buildings, unafraid of the open air behind her on the balcony, her eyes making one doubt that she would be afraid of anything. The door opened mechanically, not by means of any computer, and she was let inside with a growling sigh. "Skiya, you're late."

"Oh, hush, Devar," Skiya chuckled with a wicked grin. There were a few other people in the room, all staring out with hungry eyes and that crumb of hope that purpose creates. It was easy to live for a crumb of hope, much more difficult to live off of one. Skiya deposited the bag she carried over one shoulder onto the table, and the occupants of the room surged forwards. Devar stopped them before there could be an all-out fight and divided up the food between them. Apart from some bread, it was all raw, consisting of fruit and vegetables, a few pieces of cheese, but no prepared meals. Anything, though, was welcome, and no one cared that it wasn't the prepared food that every other citizen of the Republic received. These people were the forgotten, living by means of a few scrounged electrical lights, worn-out rags that served as clothes, food acquired by questionable methods and the words of their cause.

They had lived and starved on the Ground Level before, but Ske'toa was bringing them together. Uniting these forgotten people and giving them a place in a world where before they had none. Skiya watched as they devoured the food. Their eyes, she thought. It was in their eyes. More than emptiness, more than looking for a next meal. They had purpose. They had hope.

"Well?" Devar said, hunching over his own bit of bread and an apple. He took small bites, as if afraid that eating too quickly would upset his stomach. Or that the food would be his last. Devar was different than the others, Skiya noted. He was more aware. Maybe that was why Ske'toa trusted him almost as much as herself. Skiya perched on the edge of the table and watched the others eat without any trace of curiosity or sympathy.

"They've started whispering about the words of Ske'toa," Skiya said, her eyes gleaming, cat-like. "I heard two Watchmen who were talking about how Ske'toa took down the Interface before the Placement. The words were quoted nearabouts exactly."

"Watchmen? The news is spreading quickly," Devar said. "What were their reactions"?

"Fear. Uncertainty. The idea of the Interface being taken down was more worrisome to them than why it was done. The initial fear needs to die down for people to start discussing it." Skiya swung her legs like the child she used to be but a few short years before and scoffed. "They don't even understand what is being offered them."

"Would you expect creatures that have lived their entire lives in cages to know what to do when the door is opened?" Devar asked. Skiya raised an eyebrow as he hunched his shoulders, picking off another portion of his bread and eating it, slowly.

"You've been spending a great deal of time with Ske'toa," she noted. Curious.

"Not recently. Our leader has been too busy guiding the hands that are involved in this investigation for much personal contact with me or any of the others," Devar was wistful, admiration clear in his posture. Skiya raised her brows higher.

"Well, what do you suggest that we do? Usher these creatures, clueless as they are, out of the cages? Has Ske'toa given us directives on that count?" Skiya was fine with improvising, but something about working without Ske'toa's direct guidance was a little disconcerting. The thought sent a shiver up Skiya's spine. She gripped the edge of the table tightly.

"No," Devar replied. "We are to take initiative. Now that the motion has begun, the more contact between us, the more dangerous it is. The privacy monitors have likely already been pulling any information on people who live outside the normal…ways of society, marking us as possible rebels. Ske'toa wants us to whisper about the cause, but not loudly. The Security forces are watching."

"Ha," Skiya tossed her head. "I wouldn't worry about that. They have no proof. And I, for one, am still fully capable of avoiding those idiots in security and their pet drones. I'm a member of the Republic, didn't you know? Otherwise, how would I have gotten you that food, there?"

"You were given a false identity," Devar said flatly. "Ske'toa wanted you there to get supplies for our people. That doesn't count."

"Killjoy." Skiya rolled her eyes. She pushed herself off the table and paced before Devar. The others were listening, but only with half an ear. They were part of the cause, Skiya knew, but she didn't know their names, positions in society, or the plan. If they were here, scrounging for food, there was little doubt the Republic had already tossed them aside. Likely as not, they had barely escaped with their lives. Skiya sat beside Devar, close enough for comfort and quiet conversation. The others took the hint and huddled together in their own corner, their hungry eyes seeking out any leftover scrap of food.

Skiya looked at the floor and wondered if she should share her news. Devar was more involved in the movement, but he had also been part of the Republic. Still, his loyalty to Ske'toa was unquestionable. Skiya tucked a dark strand of hair behind her ear.

"The Watchmen were enforcing a curfew," Skiya said softly.

"What?" Devar hissed with the force of a curse. Across the room, one of the listeners flinched and Skiya narrowed her eyes. She would have taken the conversation outside, but it was far easier for the Republic to record conversation if you were out in the open rather than a protected room.

"The ones I passed, they were there to enforce a curfew. A woman had gone out to meet with some friends and was walking back to her house. They nearly arrested her because she was breaking curfew," Skiya murmured so that Devar had to strain to hear.

He made a growling noise in his chest and shook his head. "They don't want people out at night because that's when Ske'toa gets most of the work done," Devar said flatly.

"That was my guess, too," Skiya nodded. "And keeping tabs on the Dreamscape trade. Ever since our raids on the speeders, they've been trying to track down and arrest anyone even remotely close to the trade."

"That won't do any good," Devar gave half a smirk that Skiya returned two-fold. "The sellers have always been cautious. Curfews don't bother them. But even if the street supply were to vanish—"

"I know," Skiya purred. "Ske'toa makes the cause's supply. It could easily be leaked to the street vendors."

They were silent for a moment, enjoying their leader's cleverness. Even by association, it seemed, they were clever, too. They had evaded the authorities thus far and the rumours of the latest attack on the Placement centre were quickly spreading through the ranks of the Republic.

"The curfew could prove to be a problem, though." Devar sounded solemn, and the pleasure drained from Skiya's posture into one of defiance.

"I know," she nodded firmly. "If they catch any sign of us—any one of us—things could end very badly. They're looking for someone to burn for this."

"This isn't like your childhood stories of Robin Hood," Devar agreed. "If one of us gets captured, Ske'toa will do everything possible to make certain that we never see the light of day. We can't betray the cause."

"It's just a curfew," Skiya protested. Even she knew her protests were half-hearted. "No one is stupid enough to get caught. And not one of us knows enough to connect to the rest of the group."

"Doesn't matter. Curfew is just where things begin. You think that the Konsulars would trust mere Watchmen to holding a curfew? The Republic is full of cameras, full of drones and people willing to report anyone over the slightest infraction. They don't understand the cause yet, you said so yourself. You aren't just avoiding the authorities, you're avoiding every person and camera and drone. The entire Republic is going to be fighting against you."

"Isn't that what we're up against already?" Skiya snapped, just a little too loudly. The people on the other side of the room flicked their gaze to her and quickly averted it, seeing her glare. "We know what we're getting into, Devar." Skiya lowered her voice, "It's a choice we were all given and a choice we all made willingly."

"A choice for a better Republic, for a time when people will actually be able to move forwards rather than just sitting still," Devar agreed, though there was a hint of mockery in his voice. Skiya frowned; this curfew had shaken him more than she expected.

"The Republic hasn't made any technological progress since the implementation of the Interface system three generations ago. Incidentally, it was the Interface system that allowed the Placement to begin. Once people were Placed, there was no need to think any further than the immediate life right in front of you. People weren't trying to figure out problems just because they were interesting or because they wanted something better out of life. There has been no progress, only stagnation. Because people don't have to think," Skiya said. This wasn't news, but Devar hunched his shoulders.

"You think I don't know that? I don't need to be lectured by some little girl on the nature of our cause," Devar spat under his breath.

"Don't you? You seem to think that the Republic is this all-powerful thing that can catch people that don't want to be caught. You place too much faith in the technology and system of the Republic," Skiya retorted. She lifted her chin, "I made it back here through the curfew, no problem."

"I know exactly why we're doing this. I know that we are seeking choice in a time of virtual slavery. I know full well the measures that must be taken. But haven't you wondered just where Ske'toa has been this last while? We haven't had a meeting or hardly any word from Ske'toa since just before the second blackout."

"Ske'toa is busy," Skiya said. "When it is time to move or meet, we will hear about it."

"Things are beginning to heat up and—"

"You think that because there are a few Watchmen out that Ske'toa would abandon us? Only in the case of our capture, and even then, we wouldn't be abandoned," Skiya crossed her arms and kicked her legs to contain her anger. She wanted to pace, but talking with Devar required that she sit still or be overheard. "Ske'toa would come for us."

"To kill us," Devar said lowly.

"You bastard," Skiya snarled, lashing out and striking Devar on the cheek. He caught her wrist a fraction of an inch away from his face and curled his lip in a smirk.

"I am not a fool, Skiya. I know full well—and so do you—if we are caught, Ske'toa will come to kill us. Escape would be nearly impossible, and the Republic has methods of making us talk. Ending our life would be the only viable choice."

"You make it sound as though it's dirty." Skiya pulled her wrist away from Devar and cradled it in her other hand, her eyes watching his face resentfully.

"It is far from that." Devar lowered his hands to his lap and shrugged. "We all made a choice with full knowledge of the potential outcome when we joined Ske'toa. We chose to end our lives in the instance of capture rather than have to choose to give up our cause to the Republic or endure torture."

"And yet you think that Ske'toa has abandoned us because we haven't had a meeting in a while," Skiya murmured.

"I think that it's been a rather long time since we've had any direction as to which way to strike next," Devar said.

Skiya took a deep breath and let it out through her teeth, staring at the floor while thinking.

"We could talk to people. Make them wonder about the attack on the Placement. Start spreading questions about why the Republic won't let anyone move in any direction once they're put somewhere. Ask why individual uniqueness and innovation don't exist anymore. You said Ske'toa wants us to whisper," Skiya said, her voice barely a breath. She had moved her eyes on the figures across the room and was watching them as they sat, pulling their rags of clothing tighter, staving off a cold that wasn't there.

"Will people even know the meaning of those words?" Devar asked.

Skiya straightened and flashed Devar a grin. "I know what to do," she said. "Introduce the meanings. Spread data about the words that matter. Individuality. Innovation. Freedom. Choice. All of those things."

"We're nowhere near as capable at taking over the Interface as Ske'toa," Devar pointed out.

Skiya flapped her hand. "I'm capable," she said. "But I was thinking something a little more…permanent. Something that the Interface wouldn't scrub as soon as it gained control."

"Oh? And what did you have in mind?"

"Papers. Flyers. Spread all over Kyper, dropped from speeders, scattered all over the ground. People will pick them up—no one uses papers anymore, so they'll want to know what it is—and our message will be spread all over the city." Skiya tossed her head and preened with pride at her idea.

"Individuality. Innovation." Devar looked mildly impressed. "Skiya, you are the embodiment of Eloaech."

"I know," she grinned. In a flash of movement, she pushed herself away from Devar and lunged across the room, grabbing one of the other people by the shoulder. It was a man, thin and scrawny, not from hunger, though, with wide eyes and a cut across one lip. He squeaked in fear when Skiya grabbed him and practically fainted when she drew her face close to his. "Did you know that this room is protected against listening devices? And any outgoing transmissions of any kind?"

"I, uh, I—"

"Skiya, what are you doing"? Devar rose and walked over to the others, looking more than a little annoyed at the interruption in their planning. "Leave the creature alone."

"And let him take his information about us and our plans back to the Konsulars? Or do you work for Military Intelligence? Oh, Military Intelligence, I see," Skiya bared her teeth and hissed at him. It took Devar a moment to realise that she was laughing. "Look, we've moved up in the world! I thought we were only gathering the attention of Kyper Central. But we've got a Milit in our midst."

"Are you certain?" Devar asked. His eyes showed interest, but his voice and posture betrayed nothing but resigned boredom.

"Certain as a crashed speeder," Skiya said. "I could fair hear the man trying to get his transmitter to work. Not to mention he's afraid of Ske'toa."

The man did, indeed, flinch at the mention of Ske'toa, but Devar merely laughed. "Skiya, we're all afraid of Ske'toa. Some of us mix fear with admiration, though." He crouched and stared at the man Skiya still held on the floor by his shoulder. "This one, he has no admiration. Only fear."

"And disgust," the man spat, some of the spittle landing on Devar's shoes. The bigger man growled, low and deep and, no matter that he had been trained as a Medic, meant to help heal and save lives, the look

Devar gave could have killed. The Milit swallowed and stuck his chin out as much as he could in some semblance of defiance. "To even think that such lowlifes as you exist. It's disgusting. The Republic gives everything a body could want. It gives purpose and you want to tear it down, and for what? A chance to ruin your lives with failure?"

"Or the chance to succeed," Skiya flashed her teeth again and the man curled his lip. She tightened her grip on the man's shoulders enough that her fingers dug into his flesh. Scrawny as he was, he flinched. "The Republic doesn't even give us a chance."

"Under the Republic, every person succeeds because the Republic succeeds," the man sneered, but the pride in his voice was quickly giving way to fear. Perhaps it was the realisation of where he was and with whom he was doing battle, or perhaps he was beginning to doubt his words, but the fear was growing. As were Skiya's and Devar's glares.

"Or everyone stagnates, and their minds are allowed to die because they don't think for themselves." Skiya slapped her hand onto the man's other shoulder, exchanging a glance with Devar. "What are we meant to do with a Milit"?

"We can't turn him loose," Devar agreed with Skiya's silent statement. "And we don't have the resources to keep him for any length of time. He would die of starvation before any use could be gotten out of him."

"Call Ske'toa," Skiya murmured. The other people, who had fled to the opposite side of the room during the recent incident, sat up with eager looks. Ske'toa, the person they had been waiting for, was going to come. This was not a meeting, this was serious and yet it meant they had a greater chance of exchanging personal words with their leader. Ske'toa was such an important person and it was so difficult to talk for any length of time with Ske'toa, or at all, depending on how crowded the meetings were. And this was just Kyper; Ske'toa had followings all over the Republic, with quiet acts of rebellion in the name of freedom perpetrated in Ske'toa's name.

"Are you crazy?" Devar snapped, making the low-level members flinch. "We can't just *call* Ske'toa."

"Why not? We were told to call if there was an emergency." Skiya rolled her eyes. She kicked the Milit in the leg, hard enough that he did his best to shuffle out of her grasp. She was still young, though, and slight, so there wasn't enough strength to do any real damage. "I think having Milit infiltrate one of our safe houses counts as an emergency."

"And now you just told him that we have multiple safe houses." Devar straightened and threw his hands up in disbelief. Skiya grinned, enjoying his frustration just a touch more than she probably should have. Well, she decided, that was what youth was for, wasn't it? Pushing boundaries and changing the world. Or, it *would be* under the *new* system.

"Oh, relax. It's not as if informing the Milit that we're far better armed and prepared than he had thought is going to do us damage. All it will do is make them look over their shoulders more often. That is if this one even escapes our grasp. Which, if you call Ske'toa, he won't." Skiya released the man and he crawled a slight distance away while she perched on the table again. He couldn't escape, anyway. "Milits don't even issue weapons to their intelligence gatherers. The door is locked with a biometric passcode, there are enough witnesses to report what happened and will happen, enough to hunt him down. Especially considering Ske'toa's skill with the Interfaces. The moment his face hits Republic cameras—which, as you pointed out, are everywhere—then he's branded a traitor, or worse."

"We could get in serious trouble for this," Devar pulled out a transmitter and set it to the frequency that could penetrate the safe-house walls.

"If it helps, I chose this course of action. You were acknowledging my free will to act in this matter and, as I don't have a transmitter, gave in to my request to call Ske'toa." Skiya waved her hand dismissively.

"That still counts as a choice," Devar sighed. "No, no, don't look at me like that. If we're going to do this, it's a choice we *both* make." He typed a few keys in the transmitter and watched it for a moment before sliding it back into the pocket of his tunic. "It is sent. Ske'toa will be here soon."

Skiya grinned at the Military Intelligence man, who was sitting in the corner with the posture of one who had only one more battle to face and it wouldn't be pleasant. "You're in for a treat, Milit. Ske'toa is *the* person to meet."

"The Republic provides everything. It is my duty to do as the Republic asks. I will not falter, I will do my duty. To work for the Republic is to work for us all," the man muttered, pulling phrases about the Republic out of the air as if the more he could defend the Republic, the less Ske'toa would be able to do.

Skiya just leaned back and laughed.

13

The Military Intelligence man sat in the corner of the room, his knees up to protect him from the leering gaze of that young girl, Skiya, and her enforcer, Devar. They had searched him and taken away his transmitter and the camera attached to his ragged tunic, both non-functioning in the safe house. Non-functioning or not, they were still his only link to the Republic, and he was feeling very, very alone. He knew that the Republic was just outside the door, mere meters away, and yet it were as though he were as far away as he could be. The moon colony would feel closer.

It got worse, though, when the other people that had been holed up in the safe house had shuffled towards Skiya and expressed wonder at when Ske'toa was to arrive. At the words, "Soon. Any minute now, actually," the man closed his eyes and hoped that the Republic would gain something from his death. He fully expected to die. He had been taught, as all intelligence people were, to withstand torture, and he was certain that he wouldn't give up a single secret. He would, as a result, die. And, hopefully, Ske'toa would be sloppy enough that evidence could be found and Ske'toa would be caught and tried.

The door opened, a brief whisper revealing the city-lit blackness of night, and someone slipped inside. The man forced himself to open his eyes and look at the face of his enemy. He saw a person clothed in black with a scarf around the face, not overly tall and neither short. This person did not appear terribly strong, but the presence filled the room nonetheless. He realised it was because everyone else there had straightened at this person's entrance and gained a gleam of near-reverence.

"I hear we have an intruder amongst our ranks," the person spoke and Skiya nodded.

"Ske'toa," she said, dipping her head differentially where a few minutes ago she had been defiant and contrary. "I found him trying to use a transmitter. He's in the corner."

Ske'toa turned and walked over to him, crouching down. He flinched and turned away. "I see. A Milit? Hmm, yes. Devar, please open the back room. I think it would be better if the two of us spoke in private."

Would this back room be screened against sound? Would the others hear him scream? He forced himself to stand rather than take the offered hand of Ske'toa. He was led into a back room furnished with a single table, a few chairs, a sideboard, all looking as though they had seen better days. Ske'toa stepped into the room with him and the door was sealed behind them.

Ske'toa turned and unwound the scarf, throwing it onto the table while rolling shoulders as if weary. The Milit man froze, his eyes widening, a sense of horror filling him. "Ah, I see you recognise me. I wondered if you would. I had rather thought that Military Intelligence considered everyone else to be below their attention. Or perhaps I have it the other way around? Perhaps nothing is below your attention."

"But you—"

"Yes," Ske'toa nodded. "I am. However, I have grown rather fond of the name that was given me. Ske'toa. It means 'malevolent spirit', but I think it sounds grand. How did I know that? Oh, the information is all over the Interface. I do have other means, as you well know."

"What is it you want?" the Milit snapped, sweat beading on his brow. The room wasn't warm but pleasantly cool. He saw the absolute calm on Ske'toa's face and, for the first time since he had infiltrated the dissident cell, he felt real fear. Not of death, but of what Ske'toa could do to him if he didn't die. If he gave in.

"I am here to offer you a choice. It is one of the main tenets of my philosophy, you know. Free will. The ability to choose for oneself how to live one's life, the chance to advance or to fail based on merit and ability, not a predetermined game based on where the Republic *needs* people. Oh, you thought the Placement was based on aptitude? My how interesting." Ske'toa smiled and sat in one of the chairs, back to the door. He could have remained standing, but something about Ske'toa's attitude suggested that it might be better if he sat. So, he sat.

"Your system will lead to complete anarchy. Everyone living as they choose, who's to say that people won't choose to kill their neighbours," he snarled.

"By having a moral society," Ske'toa shrugged. "If you make it perfectly clear that rewards are available for those who succeed and think for themselves—a better place to live, a higher title, even a more secure family—then people will seek out those rewards. Those who do not succeed, or who choose to inflict harm on other people, they will not receive rewards."

"You suggest a people policing themselves," the man said. "There has never been a society where that works. Not in all of history."

"Not in all of known history," Ske'toa pointed out. "There is much that is not in the Republic archives. At least, not for widespread knowledge. But no, I grant that you have a valid point. People, if left to their own devices, can be quite troublesome. However, I never said that you need a self-policing society. A just society, whose self-interest aligns with the interest of others, either in providing work or products or social interaction, will know right from wrong. Those who do not choose to follow the rules of a just society, who wish to take without paying for that which they took, be it material goods or the thoughts of man, should be punished."

"And, what, the Republic doesn't pay for its goods"? What was this, some sort of debate? Why was Ske'toa going along with this argument? He was doing it to forestall torture, to push his death as far away from him as he could. Ske'toa seemed to be doing it for, well, fun.

"No," Ske'toa said simply. "They demand a person's mind, body, soul and what do the people get in return?"

"Food, shelter, society," he answered just as simply. These were easy questions; he didn't understand why Ske'toa wasn't demanding more information. Information about how much Military Intelligence knew or how to gain access to their private Interface or how far his fellow intelligence gatherers had infiltrated. He had been trained to withstand torture. He hadn't been trained for this.

"And no chance to change their circumstances or create new methods of production. No chance of moving outside of their Placement, even when such a Placement may go against all of their natural inclinations, individual strengths, interests, or beliefs. Devar, you met Devar? Yes, he was a Medic. Watched a man die in emergency transit and was nearly broken by the fact that he couldn't save this man. The Republic forced him back to his job even though he no longer believed in his skills as a Medic. He is obviously capable and very intelligent. He could have pursued work elsewhere, had he been allowed, but Placement is law in the Republic and so he was forced to choose: duty to people who would force him to do something that caused him to suffer, or become an outcast."

"It is not the fault of the Republic that your friend was unable to perform his duty. Some people, no matter the Placement, have weak minds," he retorted. As soon as he said the words, he knew they were the wrong thing to say. Ske'toa's face twisted in anger for a brief flash of time, something uncontrollable and wild, before it was wrangled under control. A moment later and the calm demeanour was back, but this time the man knew it was just a mask.

"I could have you hurt very badly for saying such things about my *friends*," Ske'toa said, idly drawing circles on the table with a single finger. "But I hold that each person is entitled to an opinion. I just happen to know that yours is wrong."

"Just as I know yours is wrong"? He was suddenly filled with an insatiable desire to push Ske'toa, to see how far he could go before making the enemy break. The sweat on his head began to drip down the back of his neck.

"Ah, but you are not in possession of all the facts," Ske'toa smiled. "See, I have cultivated a rather interesting talent, one that the Republic would rather I didn't have. I am quite adept with computers. Not just computers, but the Interface itself. It's like talking to people, coaxing them and getting them to move one way or another. I'm sure you've seen some of the things I can do with this talent."

He tightened his mouth and felt his heart racing, though he didn't know why. "The blackouts."

"The blackouts were among the simpler of my acts. Getting information your Republic doesn't want me to have, that was a slightly more interesting challenge, but one I managed. And do you know what I found?"

"You're going to tell me, I'm sure," he spat.

Ske'toa sighed and nodded.

"I will tell you if you want to hear it. I don't force anyone into anything. If you don't want to hear my discoveries, then this interview is over and I shall have to consider other courses of action for dealing with your intrusion into my organisation." Ske'toa went back to drawing with a finger on the table, as if it didn't matter whether the Milit chose to listen or not.

He ground his teeth together and resisted the urge to wipe away a bead of sweat trickling near the corner of his eye. He didn't know why the effort was so immense, only that once the bead had fallen onto his tunic, he wanted to slump in exhaustion.

"I'll hear it," he said after another heartbeat.

"Very well," Ske'toa said with a firm nod. "I was exploring the means by which a Placement is decided. Genetics play a part in it, certainly, with the children who have strong bones and a predisposition towards muscle growth going towards the jobs requiring manual labour. Those jobs are mostly automated, but many of the machines have begun to break down, no new machinery has been invented or replaced since the Interfaces were put into place three generations ago. The genetics tests also look at cranial capacity and any hereditary diseases that a person may carry. The Placements, though, are mostly decided by the fact that there are certain positions open in certain areas. It has nothing to do with a person's aptitude. Children are pliable and can be made to do almost anything with the right training. Put a child before a medical textbook and tell them that this is their future and they will learn, no questions asked. *Why?* Because it was meant to be so. Why should they question this?"

"But the Interfaces look at the aptitude tests and judge a person's ability," he protested.

Ske'toa's head shook from side to side in a slow negation of his words. "The Interfaces have millions of gigabytes of data running through their heads at any given point in a day. They are given over to privacy monitors, to people running searches or talking with others, to medical procedures done by laser, to speeder navigation and any number of other things. The amount of processing power it would take to determine a *human* variable and predict where they would be best placed? It's almost impossible to imagine."

"The tests—"

"Cannot predict individual human behaviour. The number of variables, the number of choices a single person can make, the environmental conditions that sway a person, experiences that are unique to a person, not to mention the ways a person thinks about the world, is too much to process. Why do you think the Republic cannot predict the future? And yet it claims to be able to predict where a person will do best in life just by looking at a body's genetics and a couple of aptitude tests done before the frontal lobe is even close to fully developed." Ske'toa shrugged. "Even with the added computing power of the people attached to the Interfaces, it's impossible."

"If the Placement is based solely on the need to fill empty positions, then why…?" he let the words trail off, feeling that they were too close to blasphemy against the Republic. "No, no, that can't be right. The Placement has put citizens where they are best able to serve the Republic, based on their own dispositions and, and…"

"Tell me—ah, I believe in all the excitement, I have forgotten to ask your name. And I certainly won't refer to you as Citizen." Ske'toa looked apologetic and the Milit man shrugged in acceptance.

"Zensen," he said.

Ske'toa's head dipped ever-so-slightly in acknowledgement.

"A pleasure, Zensen. Do you have any siblings? A brother, perhaps?"

"Yes. Younger by two years," he replied. He shouldn't have told Ske'toa that, let alone his name. With that information, Ske'toa could—oh, what did it matter? Ske'toa could have done anything with the Interface and a mere picture of him. His name and family weren't necessary. Which meant they were relevant to the conversation.

"Very well. Take you and your brother. Raised by the same parents, in the same house, same amount of clothing, toys, resources applied to the both of you. You were likely taught by the same teacher in the same school, though two years apart. Same in just about every way, correct?"

"Well, I suppose so..."

"Ah, yes. I take it from your reluctant reply that your brother is in no way similar to you?"

"No," Zensen admitted. "He was Placed as an Architect."

"I presume his personality is quite different from your own, as well. Yes? My point exactly. Given all of the same variables, same genetics, same resources, you two should have been Placed similarly. In a mathematical equation, one like the many trillions the Interfaces deal with every day, given the same variables, you are likely to get the same result. Not with people. So how can the Interfaces possibly deal with that? It has nothing to do with aptitude. And only marginally to do with genetics. It's all about where the Republic wants you. It has nothing to do with what *you* want or where you're most likely to excel and be satisfied."

Zensen was silent for a minute, trying to mull over that revelation in his mind. He knew that he could have easily dismissed it out of hand as a lie, something clever that Ske'toa came up with to charm loyal Republic citizens like himself. But...there was that ring of truth and the unshakeable base of logic. He couldn't dismiss those words as a lie, couldn't even discount them as a slanted view of the truth. If what Ske'toa said were true, then the Republic's version of the Placement made no sense. The words seemed to bore holes in him until he had to bite his lip to keep from moaning out loud.

"If the Republic only Places people where they need them most, then why go to the trouble of saying that it's meant to be?" he asked quietly.

"If I were to say to you that you were destined, through genetics and aptitude and some hidden knowledge that only the Interfaces can understand, to be a Military Intelligence man, would you accept it? Now, take into consideration what your reaction would be if I said that my choice had absolutely nothing to do with you, but just happened to be what I needed most, what would you do?"

"I would do my duty," Zensen answered, almost too quickly to have properly considered it. Ske'toa didn't seem to mind, though, and casually raised one shoulder.

"Perhaps. But you would also resent it and wonder if you might not be better suited to something else, something that you were good at as well as wanted to do, not just what the Republic needed. The Republic says what it does about Placement, and far more than that, because it is far easier to control a population that believes it is destined to be where it is than one simply taking orders. Orders can be broken. Destiny cannot."

Zensen shifted uncomfortably in his chair and wiped his forehead with the back of his hand. It didn't help. He looked at Ske'toa with pleading eyes, desperate to understand and yet trying to think of reasons why Ske'toa was wrong. "There must be some other reason."

"Why?" Ske'toa asked, looking genuinely interested. He swallowed and hunched his shoulders nervously.

"Because, well, because if that's true then—" he broke off, unable to say any more. Zensen closed his eyes and pressed his lips together to prevent any more words from leaving his mouth. He didn't have to, though; Ske'toa finished the sentence for him.

"Then everything the Republic is built on is a lie meant to keep you from asking too many questions," Ske'toa said. "It is meant to keep you in your place."

"The Republic *can't* be like that," Zensen cried in an attempt at flat-out denial. It didn't work, as he knew it wouldn't. How can a person deny reality when it stares him in the face?

"The Republic is doing its very best to keep from degrading. There have been no new technological shifts since the implementation of the Interfaces. There have been a few modifications on small technologies, like a different design in speeders and a better holoscreen, but think about it. The Republic achieved space travel before the Interfaces, even set up a moon colony with the design of spreading out into the stars. What has it done in the last three generations? Barely maintained the travel between the moon colony and itself. The ships we have are old, falling apart. The factories are automated, but machines break down and people are needed to replace what was once done by a machine. Think about it, Zensen. The Republic is falling apart, and the Placement system is part of the cause. People aren't thinking for themselves, so the products of innovation and original thought are dying. The Republic has stalled. All because people are just taking orders. Nothing more."

Zensen lifted his head and looked Ske'toa in the eyes, all the uncertainty and fear he felt displayed plainly on his features. "And you want to change that."

"Yes. I want freedom. I want choice and the ability to think for oneself. You understand that, don't you?" Ske'toa asked, smiling and holding out a hand, as if for Zensen to take. He knew that this was a choice being presented to him. One of the first that he had ever known in his life. Take Ske'toa's hand and he could be part of something that would make the Republic great again and would keep the authorities from lying to the people like they had been. Refuse, accept the lies he had been taught as a child that made his world safe and calm but kept him from acting of his own volition, and Ske'toa would have to act.

Zensen reached out and took Ske'toa's hand, making the choice with all the conscious effort a mind can have.

14

"Language always betrays us, tells the truth
when we want to lie, and dissolves into
formlessness when we would most like to be precise."
—Jeanette Wilson

Dawes sat in his office, a place he hadn't habited much during the investigation, and felt his age. He wasn't ancient, by Republic standards. The average citizen lived to be at least one hundred and ten years, so he had a good near forty years to go. He was still feeling old.

Most of that was to do with Amaia. She was so young and grasped onto the important points of the investigation almost before he had realised they were there. She had practically created a field of study to become a Subject-expert and was more adept at a wide range of subjects than Dawes ever hoped to be. When he was talking with her, he felt younger, like his mind was racing and he could do anything. When he was on his own, at times like this, and looking over just how far they'd come in comparison to the continued assaults by Ske'toa, he just felt old.

"In nearly two weeks' time, I'm meant to be Decommissioned," Dawes murmured into the glass of amber liquid he cradled in his hand. It was the end of a long day of looking over Interface schematics, few of which made sense to him, trying to understand how Ske'toa kept taking their information out of the Interfaces and had also infiltrated the Placement centre. Amaia had called it a night just after dark and gone home, looking as weary as Dawes felt. He had returned to Kyper Central and went straight to his secret panel in the wall where he had previously kept the nanites and now kept his liquor.

In all his years at Kyper Central, Dawes had never thought that using illegal nanites made him a disloyal Citizen. Now, even the alcohol felt like a lie he had to keep. Much like the Konsulars and TechElite had done with him.

The liquor reduced the headache, but it didn't make him feel any better. Still, it was better than wallowing in his own worries, so he put the glass to his lips and tilted back his head, downing the remaining liquid in one swallow. The moment he did, his eyes still watering slightly, the door to his office slid open without any warning. Dawes was on his feet in an instant, fumbling the glass to his desk with one hand and getting out his Fyre gun with the other. Perhaps because of his age, he was too slow.

The person entering wore the deepest black tunic and trousers, a silver badge of the infinity symbol within a circle on the left breast of the tunic. The man was not tall, but well-built and commanded authority. His head was completely shaven, and he had the severe look of someone who would not bear nonsense. Dawes didn't know the man from anyone else, but the darkness in the man's eyes gave his position away, if the black tunic didn't. Coupled with the fact that he had entered Dawes' office without permission—something only those of higher security clearance than the Inspectors of Kyper Central could manage—Dawes suddenly wanted to be very, very far away.

"You are Inspector Maddox Dawes," the man said. It was not a question, not a greeting, but Dawes nodded anyways. Amazing, Dawes thought, how often the formal greeting had been dropped in recent times. By him and by others. The man took a long look at Dawes and let out a slow breath through his nose. "I see."

"Is there something I can do for Military Intelligence?" Dawes asked. The workers Placed at Military Intelligence were not to be feared for their strength or their fighting skills, for their ability to kill or anything that was physically dangerous. They were feared because of their minds: sharp, focused, with the most acute observation skills and access to any information they pleased. Only the Konsulars were above them in status, and they wielded political power more than mental power. To be faced with someone from Military Intelligence was a dangerous task, because you never knew if they were coming for you or for your help.

"One of my men has gone missing," the man said in a flat tone. Dawes blinked and raised his brow. His heart, which had started racing the moment the man entered his office, slowed. Marginally.

"I'm certain that Military Intelligence can find your—"

"He was infiltrating one of the cells belonging to your Ske'toa."

Ah. Dawes understood. He sank back into his chair and gestured to the seat across from his desk. "You may as well have a seat, then."

The Military Intelligence man sat, and Dawes ignored the look of distaste that his guest bore. "What you need to know is that we had come across some information, smuggled to us by a worker who overheard two others talking about somewhere they could meet with others who sought more space under the current regime. He has gone missing. He infiltrated the cell over a period of three months—"

"But that's before any of the Ske'toa attacks," Dawes interrupted. The man frowned but nodded.

"Yes. This was part of an ongoing task to seek out and capture all parties that fall under dissident allegiance. It is one of the many directives belonging to Military Intelligence." The man, obviously a higher-up in the organisation, brushed an imaginary speck of dust from his trousers before crossing his ankle over his knee. The casual gesture—part of kinesics, the study of body movements as taught to him by Amaia—was more threatening than friendly.

"I see," Dawes said. "So, your agent infiltrated the cell and has gone missing. Could he simply be unable to contact you?"

"All of our agents are fitted with micro-transmitters that inform us of their whereabouts twenty-four hours a day. His stopped transmitting last night. It started again this morning and, when we went to inquire as to the reason for its failing, we found the transmitter tacked to a wall underneath the words: *Ta Eloai. Ta chi kai.*"

"I am a Wanderer. I am free," Dawes translated. He shook his head and squeezed the bridge of his nose, groaning under his breath.

"You know these words"?

"I'm working with a linguist who has been teaching me this language…it's the language these dissidents use, in order to associate them with an ancient peoples, the Eloai. Wanderers. *Ta* is the first-person pronoun, I, also indicative of the present tense in this case because there is no verb to be in the present tense…" Dawes trailed off. The man made no move to show interest, but Dawes had the unsettling feeling that everything he said was being considered and analysed and cataloged for future reference.

The Military Intelligence man blinked slowly, but that was the only sign that he had cared about Dawes' words. He looked around the office a moment before slipping his hand into his tunic pocket and pulled out a data crystal. He slid across the desk.

"What's this?" Dawes asked.

"The information on my agent's whereabouts before the transmitter went dead and up until the time it was found by us," the man said.

Dawes coughed as though he had swallowed more alcohol and stared, wide-eyed at the man.

"You want me to investigate his disappearance"?

"Don't be ridiculous. I want you to investigate his disappearance only as another piece of information to be considered in the Ske'toa investigation." The man lifted his chin defensively and stared at Dawes as if daring him to challenge his statement.

"Why doesn't Military Intelligence investigate? Surely you have the authority to take over from here, and a personal interest now that your man's gone missing." Dawes wanted to reach out and snatch the crystal, realising just what it could mean in the investigation, but he held back. For what, understanding? A month ago, he would have just taken the crystal and gone about his job. No, Dawes corrected, he probably still would have asked. It was one of those things about him that his superiors and others around K.C. found particularly annoying. Dawes liked asking 'why'.

"We gather information and observations. We do not investigate." The way the man said it made Dawes feel as if his job had been sneered at. He imagined that if this man didn't need him, they would never have met. It was too far out of the Placement strata for comfort. If only Dawes cared about his comfort.

"You will have to understand that what I do and find with this information is to remain under Kyper Central control. This is *my* case. I am the one who is going to find and take Ske'toa down, and I don't care what sort of powerplays you have in mind. Once I take this crystal, you walk out of this office with no more say in things than you had before you came," Dawes growled. Maybe it was the drink or maybe it was him feeling his age. He thought it likely that it was more to do with the upcoming Decommissioning. He had to finish this before then or it would be postponed. He wasn't sure he would take that.

"I understand," the man said flatly, his eyes betraying his dislike. He rose and left the office without another word or backwards glance. Dawes waited until he was gone before snatching the crystal up and grinning like a bandit.

He nearly slipped the crystal into the port on his desk before pausing. He could look at the data, but he would have to run an Interface program to analyse it, and things hadn't ended well when trying to do that recently. All of his data, carefully input at the end of each day, went missing. Placement centres had been attacked. Ske'toa had taken over the city twice already. If he wanted to analyse the data, he was going to do it without an Interface. Luckily for him, he knew someone who was quite good at analysing data.

"Tell me again why you're at my house at nearly midnight?" Amaia yawned. Dawes hadn't bothered to call her before showing up at her quarters. She lived with other subject-experts and teachers from the University in a commune that was, by Kyper standards, fairly nice. The building was tall and thin, and each dwelling had a large bathroom, separate bedroom, study and living space with food storage. Amaia sat at her table with a cup of cocoa she had ordered from Food Preparation. She had demanded that Dawes wait to tell her anything until her cocoa arrived.

Dawes explained what had happened with the Military Intelligence man and Amaia sat up straighter. She looked ready to jump right in, despite the dressing gown and slightly mussed hair. Dawes envied her youth, wondering what it would be like to work again as if he had no weariness in his bones, as if he weren't looking at every moment of this case behind the goal of his Decommissioning. He needed to get this done. That was what drove him. Amaia was driven by her curiosity and desire to learn. That hurt.

"You have the data?" she asked.

Dawes held out the crystal and barely refrained from flinching when she snatched it from his hand, their skin touching. He shouldn't feel jealousy, he knew. There was no point. But the jealousy was there. He would have, at that very moment, given anything to feel as invigorated about the case as she did. He wanted to feel the sort of passion that pushed her, rather than this need to find Ske'toa merely to finish his career. She was looking for a next step in her life; he was looking for a way out.

A brief moment flashed in Dawes' mind, one in which he stayed on past his Decommissioning, continuing to do good at Kyper Central, not because his ability was destined by the Republic, but because he was good at his work. He could take personal pride in his successes, not because he had done his duty, but because he did it well. The thought vanished as the data crystal left his palm. Dawes was left with nothing more than that initial flash of jealousy and a weight in his shoulders he had almost forgotten was there.

Amaia slid the crystal into her computer port and waved her hands, each twitch sifting through the data until the holographic display showed exactly what they needed. A map of the district in Kyper where the Military Intelligence agent had last been tracked and where his tracker had reappeared pulsated lightly in the darkness of the room.

"I thought you didn't use computers," Dawes said, surprised at how quickly and ably she had gotten the computer to do what she wanted. Her movements were expert and far more subtle than his own broad movements.

"Most of my field has to do with data of all sorts. Live conversations, text, streams, video recordings, not just books and archival data. My work with you, learning Eloaech, has been mostly book-bound, simply because there is no information to be had in computers." Amaia pulled her dressing robe tighter around her as she looked at Dawes through the hologram. "Just because I use books doesn't mean I don't know how to use computers."

"So I see," Dawes said, impressed. He pointed to the display. "Where is this"?

"One of the factory districts, I think." Amaia spread her fingers and the map grew, turning so that they were better able to see it. "If this is correct—and given your source, I imagine it is—then…well, surely I don't need to tell you the implications."

"Given that this agent's tracker appeared with the choice Eloaech phrases that our dissidents use, then I would say he's been taken by Ske'toa." Dawes nodded.

Amaia held up a finger, "Not taken. Joined. He said, 'I am free', not 'he is free', which suggests voluntary joining, not coercion."

"The fact that Ske'toa has the ability to convince a Military Intelligence agent to join up is marginally terrifying," Dawes muttered.

Amaia nodded, looking thoughtful.

"But the time that the tracker was offline is probably when it was taken out."

"I doubt it. Those trackers are meant to work under just about any type of strain. Their specifications went around some of the technology labs at the University and they were whistling over the new modifications for a while. That means the tracker had to be in a place where the signal couldn't get through," Amaia said.

She was watching Dawes closely enough that he felt as though he should be the one doing more of the talking. She kept displaying her wide range of knowledge, and it was embarrassing. He was the Inspector. He should have been able to put the puzzle pieces together. "A signal-free house. A Hush House, they're called," he growled. "Illegal, naturally, but that wouldn't stop Ske'toa."

"Then this agent was in the 'Hush House'. Probably with Ske'toa," Amaia said, a smile growing on her face. Whether she was oblivious to his emotional turmoil or just pointedly ignoring it, he couldn't tell. He was grateful either way.

"The point where the tracker went offline is the Hush House. That's Ske'toa's. Or at least it belongs to the dissidents, if not where they're based," Dawes began to grin, too. He no longer cared that it was past midnight or that he was about to wake his superior on what might potentially turn into a wild goose chase. He just held out his hand to Amaia through the display, the map wavering around his arm. "Let's go get Ske'toa."

"You had better be right about this, Maddox," Daleni Itar said through his earpiece. He kept a straight face as he strapped the light armour on and looked at the Kyper Central strike team around him. "I've called in some serious favours to get this done on the sly. If this fails, my head is on the line. This investigation has already gone on for too long."

"Understood," was all that Dawes said, but he felt like cheering. *Far too long?* It was almost done. He knew where Ske'toa had been, where people allied with that person were quartered. He was going to go in there and take them down. And in two weeks, he would be Decommissioned, no thought of dissidents or words floating around his head. He faltered for a moment. The dissidents would surely be gone; he could care less about them. The words, on the other hand, never seemed to go away. Ever since he had been schooled in their meanings, intended meanings, subtleties, uses and, above all, choices, Dawes noticed them more and more. Noticed what he chose to say and to whom, what people said to him and others. It was constantly in his head and, Decommissioning or no, would always be in his head.

"Let's go," a hardened-looking woman on the team said. Dawes nodded, lowered his visor, and stepped up to the door of the Hush House. It was nothing more than another room in the commune of the factory workers. There were no distinguishing marks to tell it from its neighbours except that its number was one-thirty-seven, not one-thirty-six or one-thirty-eight. That was all. But that was where this would end.

With a shout and a wave of his hand, Dawes disabled all security on the door and barrelled in, gun raised to shoot and stun anyone in the room. There was nothing there. The strike team streamed in behind him and searched the place thoroughly. They found the back room and even went so far as to look in the ceiling tiles and bathroom ventilation. Nothing. The only furniture was a single chair with a piece of folded paper on it.

Dawes lowered his gun and stepped towards to the chair, his heart pounding in his ears, shouting at him for his failure. He picked up the paper and, barely registering the fact that his name was written on it, opened it.

> *Congratulations, Inspector*, it began, the letters neatly
> typed and mocking. *You have done exceptionally well in getting
> this far. You have utilised your resources and used reason and
> logic in your quest to find me, which I commend. Unfortunately,*

Inspector, I am not quite ready to be brought in. I have a few things yet to do. I will tell you this: no machine could have determined that you would be such a capable Inspector, so dogged and intelligent. That, Inspector Maddox Dawes, was your choice. What you choose to do next will be highly interesting to see.

Yours truly,

Ske'toa

Dawes didn't realise he was crushing the paper in his fist until he could close his fingers no farther. He shook with rage and hurled the paper as far away from him as he could, watching with furious dissatisfaction when it fell lightly to the ground. Dawes let out a roar of anger. He didn't notice the strike team stepping back from him, exchanging glances uncertainly. All he did was point at the paper, snarling.

"Let me tell you this, Ske'toa," Dawes hissed. "I will bring you down if I have to spend the rest of my life doing it. This has nothing to do with duty or the Republic. This will be *my choice.*"

Across the city, in a darkened room where everything in that Hush House could be watched remotely, Ske'toa leaned back in a chair and smiled. "Very good, Inspector," Ske'toa murmured. "You're learning."

15

Daleni Itar tugged at her tunic as she walked towards the Konsular's office. She walked with straight back and straight face, yet neither made her feel any better. This was not a reprimand for not following through on filing a report or for disregarding training. This was the end of her career. Her work for the Republic was going to end, no matter that she had done her duty. For some people, it would never be good enough, and they were eventually cast aside by the Republic.

She raised her hand and knocked on the door, doing her best to look calm. The door slid open and she stepped inside the office. It was far nicer than the one she had as Head of Kyper Central and certainly better than those of the Inspectors she oversaw. She recalled the day when she had been promoted, how she had stared at her office. Her Placement had put her at Kyper Central, giving the extra option for advancement. It was a fairly common statement; most people were Placed with the option for advancement. The decision for advancement, for her promotion, had not come from the Interface who had given her the option, but from the Konsulars. She didn't need a machine to tell her she had failed. Badly.

"Greetings, Citizen. Please, have a seat," the Konsular waved his hand grandly. Daleni Itar recognised him as the one involved in the incident at the Placement centre, a Konsular Ramani. This was the one who had contacted her about Dawes and the Dreamscape. Who had informed her, in no uncertain terms, that if things did not go well with this investigation that she would be the one to pay the price. The Republic could not have dissidents. And Dawes' encounter—or lack thereof—at the Hush House meant the dissidents continued.

Daleni Itar sat in the chair opposite his desk, rubbing her hands along the arms. She looked down in surprise and ran her hands over the chair again.

"Yes," Ramani nodded. "It is real wood."

"I didn't even know they made real wood furniture anymore," Daleni Itar said, amazed at the feel of the grain under her fingers. "I thought everything was synthetics nowadays."

"I had that restored from the Archives," the Konsular said, a note of pleasure in his voice. "The extra material was not easy to find, but apparently the moon colony has had good luck in planting forests."

Daleni Itar nodded, wishing she could enjoy the luxury of the Konsular's office more. Instead, she kept silent, her eyes watching Konsular Ramani while her hands ran over the wood of the chair, marking it as something solid and real.

"You know why I have summoned you here," Ramani said, his voice low. He folded his hands across his chest and raised his eyebrows expectantly.

Daleni Itar swallowed and nodded again. Summoned, she thought. How appropriate.

"Have you anything to report on the investigation? Any news as to the whereabouts of this Ske'toa character or the capture of the dissidents?"

Daleni Itar knew that Ramani already knew the answer. After Dawes' failure the night before, she had known full well what would happen. Dawes had been one step behind Ske'toa and someone needed to be blamed for it. Dawes couldn't be held responsible, as he was the only one who seemed to be actually getting anywhere near Ske'toa—for goodness sake, he had been addressed openly in that note by Ske'toa—and no one could take *his* place. She wanted to curse him for his doggedness. It was what made him a great Inspector, but it was infuriating, sometimes, and bought him no allies. It did bring him results. That was what the Konsulars cared about. Daleni Itar straightened her shoulders and blinked back tears at what she knew was about to happen. "No," she said, her voice barely more than a whisper.

Ramani nodded, his expression impersonal. He didn't care that her entire life was about to be taken from her. Not literally, but if she didn't have her career, if she couldn't do her duty to the Republic, as she was Placed to do, then what did she have? The pain centred in a knot just behind her clavicle. She rubbed the spot, trying to make the ache go away.

"I see," he said flatly. "In that case, it is my prerogative to inform you that the governing body of the Republic feels that you are not adequately performing your duty to the Republic. You have failed the charge of your Placement. As the Republic requires that every citizen do his or her duty to uphold the standards of living and the morality of duty to the Republic that provides food, shelter, society, peace, your failure to complete this essential task is a failure to the Republic. Therefore, by order of the Office of the Konsulars and signed by the Head of the Republic himself, you are being stripped of your Placement."

Daleni Itar couldn't prevent her shoulders from shaking and tears leaking from her eyes. In this moment, when all she needed was a straight face so she could cry later, in private, her very willpower was failing her. Maybe she deserved this.

It wasn't Dawes' fault that Ske'toa was so far ahead and seemed to know everything. Kyper Central was responsible for bringing down Ske'toa and all associated dissidents, but Kyper Central had failed. *She* had failed. She should have put more personal effort into this investigation instead of sitting behind her desk, waiting for Dawes to come to her with answers. She shouldn't have paced her office, waiting for his call. She shouldn't have bothered with menial reports from other Inspectors. She hadn't done her duty. Because of that, the entire Republic would suffer. Konsular Ramani was justified.

That didn't make her weeping anger any less. Her shame, however, increased.

Daleni Itar had stopped listening to Ramani, unable to bear hearing the official words that were stripping her of everything she had ever known. She would be sent to the Rabesh Colony and join a work camp, where her duty to the Republic could still be fulfilled. It was humiliating, full of people who had failed and could do nothing more but lift rocks or sort through slag. It was a place where no one was anyone. No one cared about you there. You worked until you died and you were forgotten long before then. It was the place of her nightmares.

She remembered that she had growled at Dawes early on in the investigation, stating that she wouldn't stand to be sent to Rabesh. Yet there she was, her shoulders shaking and tears flowing freely, her mouth contorted in a grimace while Konsular Ramani looked on in distaste. He waved his hand over the computer terminal and a document appeared on the display.

"Press your hand to the terminal to show that you acknowledge your shortcomings and the actions the Republic must take on your account to maintain the integrity of the society in which we all live," Ramani droned, the words seemingly no more important to him than a recitation of a lunch order. To Daleni Itar, they spelled the doom of her existence.

How could the same words mean two entirely different things to different people? They spoke the same language, knew the meaning of those words, how they were strung together in that sentence, but they were hearing two different things. Did circumstance, social Placement, and individual perspective matter that much?

Daleni Itar thought about the linguist Dawes had brought into the investigation to help decipher the language of the dissidents. Obviously, she thought as she placed her shaking hand on the computer terminal, those things mattered an awful lot. If they didn't, then maybe she would have been able to accept her fate as the best course of action for the Republic. She might have been as cool and collected as Konsular Ramani, determining what was best for everybody by stripping her of her Placement. Daleni Itar wasn't cool or collected, and she wanted to spit at the fact that Ramani was only looking out for the Republic.

So what if she had failed? It was one mistake over the course of her career, not being as involved as she should have been. And the Republic was punishing her for it. Shouldn't she be supported? Shouldn't she be given a second chance, or the ability to choose where she would go from there.

No. Daleni Itar hunched her shoulders and rubbed her hands together, suddenly cold. The Republic was law. Her duty had not been fulfilled and she was going to pay for it. And that was all there was.

Daleni Itar didn't bother saying farewell to the Konsular. She stood and left his office, her dark face tear-streaked and a mess. She ignored his look of distaste and the disdainful gaze of all those she passed in the hallway leading to the speeder bay. She just hugged her arms close to herself and sobbed, each heartbeat too loud in her ears. Daleni Itar ordered her speeder home and then collapsed, her mind full of the horrors that awaited her at Rabesh. Those who failed the Republic deserved to be punished. She had heard many things about Rabesh and each of the rumours only made her feel worse.

She knew she had failed. Shouldn't she accept her punishment as something she deserved? Daleni Itar paced around her home, ignoring the sight of the shining city of Kyper outside the windows. She deserved it, it was her fault. This Ske'toa was an abomination. It was her responsibility to catch and deliver such abominations to the justice system. She failed. She failed to guide Dawes. She failed to push the investigation forwards. All her growling and snarling had just covered up ineptitude.

Daleni Itar found she couldn't face fulfilling her duty to the Republic in the work colony of Rabesh. She couldn't face living amongst others who had failed. She couldn't face being forgotten, her name stripped from the Republic as though she had never been. There was nothing for her at Rabesh. She had years to act on her duty to the Republic, but the shame and the anger were overwhelming. Such a high Placement and look where she was now, standing on the balcony as she stared out unseeing over Kyper.

"I'm sorry," she whispered, her voice catching in her throat. "I can't. I can't."

Daleni Itar knew she was making a choice that was selfish and completely disregarded the will of the Republic. She didn't care. "Just call it one more failure!" she cried out into the afternoon-blue sky. No speeders stopped and no one called her computer, telling her she was wrong. It didn't feel wrong, not anymore. She leaned over the balcony and took one deep breath, her eyes fixed on the tall, grey building she could see in the distance: Kyper Central.

"I would have given you everything," she breathed, "of my own free will, if you had let me choose how to go. Goodbye, Citizens."

Knowing that was not how the Republic functioned, Daleni Itar took her revenge and let go of the railing, leaning farther over the balcony. A moment later, she was gone.

16

"Dawes, I'm so sorry," Amaia said, sitting across from him in his office.

He looked at her blankly, not quite sure what she was doing there. Hadn't they already failed to capture Ske'toa? Hadn't he run out of ideas as to how to find this rebel leader? There was certainly no new scrap of language for her to pour over. He blinked and stared down at his desk before it occurred to him that she could be talking about the suicide of Daleni Itar.

The Republic authorities had reported in all the appropriate news outlets that it was an unfortunate accident, but Dawes had been an Inspector for too long to believe that. If it had been an accident, the safety nets on the balconies over the entire level of Daleni Itar's commune would have been out of order, not deliberately disabled. She had taken down the protection herself. Her biometric signature was on the computer. There was no doubt in Dawes' mind that Daleni Itar had killed herself.

The general population believed, though, that it was an unfortunate accident. The rumours around Kyper Central varied between Daleni Itar being unable to cope with her responsibilities, now that a serious threat to the Republic—meaning Ske'toa—had arisen, or the more popular belief that Ske'toa had gotten to her. If Ske'toa could make a Military Intelligence agent switch sides, why couldn't Ske'toa also instill despair into the Head of Kyper Central?

Personally, Dawes wouldn't have been surprised if Ske'toa had figured out a way to get to Daleni Itar; he just didn't think that Ske'toa was responsible. What would the leader of the rebels gain by pushing her towards suicide? The Konsulars would merely take over running K.C. until a new Head could be appointed. Dawes would still investigate. Nothing would change.

"Dawes, are you even listening to me?" Amaia asked.

He blinked and realised that she had been talking. He shrugged noncommittally.

Amaia took a deep breath, looking more determined than usual. Her sympathy seemed to have vanished while he had stopped listening. "I was asking why she had killed herself."

"Why would you think I know?" Dawes asked. He wanted to say it with his usual snap, but all that came out was a flat, uninterested tone. He was interested, he supposed, it was just that *this* on top of his failure two nights ago to apprehend Ske'toa was making him tired of the whole thing.

"Well, you were in communication with Daleni Itar after the attempt at the Hush House," Amaia said. "Did she seem depressed to you"?

Dawes considered, forcing himself to think and answer Amaia's questions. If nothing else, it would push away this dreadful feeling of pointlessness. "She was angry," Dawes said. That was something of an understatement. Daleni Itar had been furious, her eyes bulging as she snarled insults at Dawes' capabilities. "She said that I was obviously incompetent if a half-brained dissident could see me coming. She said that the Konsulars were not pleased, and I was lucky that this hadn't been publicised, like some of the Konsulars wanted, or it would be a whole lot worse for me. She said that my failure reflected on the whole of Kyper Central and that she would have to deal with it."

Amaia let out a low gasp. Dawes straightened in his chair and raised his eyebrows. "That's it," she said.

"What is? Daleni Itar yelling at me is nothing new. She's been complaining about my lack of progress and demanding constant updates on anything we found, so she could report it to the Konsulars and keep out of the Rabesh Colony," Dawes shrugged.

"They blamed her," Amaia said, voice quiet and eyes shining with something akin to feverish excitement. "Don't you see? She wasn't yelling at you because you were incompetent, she was yelling at you because another failure meant that someone would have to be blamed. The Konsulars need someone to explain why we've failed so far to catch Ske'toa. Daleni Itar was that person."

"She was only involved in the investigation as a supervisor, just like always. She never got directly involved unless it was a recent Placement who needed training. I was just meant to report to her as soon as I found something," Dawes shook his head. "Why would the Konsulars bother blaming her"?

"Well, they couldn't blame you," Amaia said as though it were obvious. "You're still needed to find Ske'toa. I'm only here as a consultant and there isn't really anyone else *to* blame."

"So—what, Daleni Itar killed herself because she was blamed for not finding Ske'toa?" Dawes snorted. "She would never be so weak. Her duty to the Republic was much stronger than that."

"You said it yourself, Daleni Itar was afraid of being sent to the Rabesh Colony. That is the punishment for a citizen who is found unable to do their duty to the Republic. Criminals get other sentences, but the lazy and incapable get sent to Rabesh," Amaia leaned forwards, eyes shining. "I'd venture a guess that Daleni Itar was removed as Head of Kyper Central and ordered to Rabesh Colony for failure to complete her duty. She killed herself instead."

"That's an even greater breach of duty," Dawes curled his lip, disgusted at the thought of his superior acting in such a manner. "To deprive the Republic of able work and shirking duty is one of the worst crimes a person can commit. It…it's just wrong. Daleni Itar would never do such a thing."

"Unless she chose not to go to Rabesh. After being Head of Kyper Central, can you imagine the shame?" Amaia shuddered.

Dawes pushed back from his desk and folded his arms defensively. "All of this talk about choice, it's all stemming from Ske'toa. Why couldn't this person stay quiet? Why couldn't they have just kept to themselves and left the rest of us alone? We were happy! Now things are becoming tense between the Konsulars and K.C. and the general populace is spouting rumours of Ske'toa's doings and what it might mean. Everything was fine before!"

"Was it?" Amaia asked softly, tilting her head slightly. "Or was Ske'toa just bringing to light something the Republic wanted to keep hidden"?

Dawes narrowed his eyes, unable to believe the words he was hearing. "Are you taking their side in all of this? Perhaps all that language studying has made you too interested in what Ske'toa has to say."

Now it was Amaia's turn to curl her lips. "So now I'm a rebel? One of those dissidents that you would love to kill on sight? All I've been doing is asking questions and trying to understand what Ske'toa wants. I've been analysing words and messages and tearing apart every instance of communication we have in order to understand Ske'toa's motives and I've asked questions that no one in the Republic even wants to ask. It's nice to know your opinion of me, Inspector."

She rose and turned to leave his office, her shoulders thrown back in outrage. Dawes quickly stood, "Amaia, wait!"

She turned, her eyes burning though the rest of her was calm. Dawes froze, unable to think. Dawes saw her beauty, then, as something that took time to be understood but was definitely there. It had taken him so long to understand her mind and he wasn't even sure that he understood it at all. That was, probably, part of Amaia's allure. He wanted to spend time with her, not as a man to woman, but mind to mind. And there she was, staring at him with fire in her eyes, a spectacular example of the capability of people. Dawes couldn't find the words in his head to apologise, though he longed to do so. He couldn't do anything but stare, hoping she understood what his eyes were trying to say. Amaia scoffed and shook her head, turning back to the door.

Moments later, she was gone.

Dawes sank into his chair and let out a shuddering breath. The one time he needed words, they failed. Ironic, he supposed, considering Amaia's Placement. He waved his hand in front of the compartment in the wall and pulled out the decanter and glass. The amber liquid was running low, but Dawes imagined that it would be enough to get him drunk. If nothing else, he would get a pleasant buzz. For a moment, he understood why Konsular Ramani took Dreamscape. Dealing with all of the unpleasant emotions that this investigation had stirred up was overwhelming. Nothing in his entire career had prepared him for this.

He poured out a glass and drank that down quickly, hoping it would alleviate some of the discomfort. All it did was burn slightly going down, so he poured out another glass and drank that, too. Feeling slightly better, Dawes leaned back in his chair and allowed himself to nurse the third glass. He had closed his eyes and was on the point of falling asleep when the female voice of his computer spoke. "Call from Konsular Salesh Ramani," she intoned. Dawes opened his eyes and stared at the ceiling. He sighed and put the glass and decanter back into their hiding spot.

"Answer," he said, just as the computer was about to repeat her message.

"Hello, Citizen. Inspector Dawes," Ramani's voice was smooth and relaxed and Dawes imagined that, just like himself, Ramani had taken something to keep the horrors away. To think that he had been so disgusted when first discovering what Ramani and the other Konsulars did in taking Dreamscape. He, himself, wouldn't venture that far, but in certain circumstances, taking the edge off was exactly what Dawes needed.

"Konsular," Dawes lifted his head so he could see the hologram of Ramani across from his desk. "What can I do for you"?

"Has there been any news on Ske'toa," Ramani asked. Dawes scoffed openly and shook his head.

"Not a whisper," he growled. It seemed that along with his disgust, his respect had also vanished. He recognised that this man had considerable amounts of authority, which Dawes would never be able to match, but the deferential fear and respect Dawes had held was gone. "But you already knew that. I've been funnelling my reports to your office, so you should know exactly what hasn't been going on. Unless you have information?"

"I don't," Ramani said, sounding distinctly less relaxed than he had a moment ago. The fact made Dawes smirk and he raised his eyebrows expectantly. "You know the situation regarding Daleni Itar"?

"I know that she's dead. And that she killed herself. Some people think that Ske'toa was involved, but I think that it was probably just incompetence on your part," Dawes leaned back in his chair again to look at the ceiling. Amaia's words regarding what probably happened to Daleni Itar made more and more sense. Did he actively blame the Konsulars, no, but somebody had obviously fallen through on their duties and responsibility. "Unless you're determined to pretend that it's the accident the news outlets have been trumpeting all day"?

"No," Ramani snapped. Dawes was glad he wasn't looking at the man's face; he didn't care to see the effect his words were having. "The problem is that the general populace doesn't believe the news outlets. Along with the rumours of Ske'toa's doings, apparently there have been discussions about the governing policy of the Republic. It has caused serious disturbances. The Watchmen set to enforce the curfew have been assaulted twice, not by dissidents but by people who were determined to go out in the evening."

"I see," Dawes said drily. "And you think that my miraculously pulling Ske'toa out of the air will solve all your problems. Well, I hate to break it to you, but that is incredibly unlikely, unless the fool decides to walk into my office and surrender."

"I am not asking for a miracle," Ramani said, "nor do I expect you to find Ske'toa any time soon. The rebel has proven to be rather, hmm, difficult to apprehend."

"Then what do you want"?

"I want you to appear beside the Konsulars in a widely-broadcast discussion in order to dispel the rumours regarding Daleni Itar and the blasphemous ideas that Ske'toa has been spreading about the city," Ramani said. Dawes sat up straight and stared at the projection of the

Konsular in dismay.

"You want me to do *what?* That's not my job. That's for Konsulars and journalists and Public Relations managers and—"

"You will do this, Inspector," Ramani hissed, his eyes narrowing to dangerous slits. The Dreamscape must be wearing off, Dawes figured. "You are the only one who understands Ske'toa's ideas and methods enough to discuss them at any length. You will meet me at the Interface centre located at the base of the Konsular offices this evening at seven. This is an essential act on your part to ensure your duty to the Republic is fulfilled during this difficult time. Do I make myself clear?"

Dawes stared hopelessly at the projection. If he thought that investigating a language was out of his Placement, talking to large crowds at length about an ideology he only understood with the help of someone else was going to be a complete disaster. The holographic projection of the Konsular waited only for Dawes to nod numbly before vanishing. Dawes, for his part, was torn between wanting to hit the wall until his hands bled and finishing off his drink. He was going to need his head clear, he decided, and stood to beat the wall when a third option came to him. He would have to go after Amaia. She understood Ske'toa better than he did and she was intimately aware of the power of language. If anyone could speak before a large audience, it would be she.

Dawes rose from his desk and grabbed his coat, ordering a speeder and hoping that she would be where he thought she was. He ordered the speeder to the University and didn't even bother knocking, expecting his Kyper Central authorisation to get him through the door. What he didn't expect was that Amaia would be laying on the floor, her hands folded neatly over her stomach, feet crossed, eyes wide and staring unseeing at the ceiling.

Dawes cursed and rushed over to her. "Amaia? Are you alright? Are you hurt? Please tell me you're not dead!"

She blinked and sat up on her elbows. "What?! Why would you think I'm dead?"

"You were laying on the floor..."

"I do that when I need to think. Or when I'm too lazy to spread a blanket out on the couch." She frowned, narrowing her eyes, "Are you here to arrest me?"

"Why would I arrest you"? Dawes sat on the floor out of sheer relief, not even caring that the chair was a few feet away. Amaia was alright. Things were going to be alright.

"Because you've obviously decided that I'm working with Ske'toa," Amaia said with a sniff.

"You're not working with Ske'toa," Dawes said firmly. "You're working with me. And I need your help tonight."

"For what? Another raid? Have you gotten wind of something Ske'toa has planned?" Amaia sat up properly this time and watched Dawes with interest.

"Konsular Ramani is hosting a discussion this evening that is to be broadcast anywhere Ske'toa's rumours have reached. I'm meant to be explaining away Ske'toa's ideas and making certain that no one could misconstrue them as beneficial in any way," Dawes said. He scowled, "Apparently I'm the only one who understands Ske'toa enough to make such a speech."

"And you want me to help you? You know as much as I do," Amaia shrugged. Dawes shook his head.

"I don't," he pressed. "I know a little, enough to explain what it is Ske'toa thinks, generally speaking. You *understand* what it is Ske'toa is trying to say. But not only that, you're a linguist."

Amaia blinked. "What does that have to do with anything? You want me to go into the finer points of Eloaech? Because I could, but your audience would be asleep before I got to conjugating the first-person plural verbs."

"No, no, you understand words. You understand language and speaking and different words for different situations. You know how to talk to a large group of people." Dawes looked at Amaia and saw her eyes widen, though whether in shock or flattery, he wasn't sure. He was fairly certain that her astonished laughter couldn't be good.

"You want me to do the speech for you," she said, still laughing, "because you think that I know how to talk to large groups of people due to the fact that I'm a linguist."

Dawes drew his brows together. This was not going as he had hoped; he had wanted Amaia to accept his apology and immediately agree to help him. Not laugh at his ideas. "Yes," he snapped. "I fail to see what's so funny."

"You misunderstand the point of linguistics completely." Amaia shook her head, chuckling. "Being a linguist and understanding how language works and being able to deconstruct a situation to analyse its language components has nothing to do with my ability to speak in front of crowds. One involves analytics, the other charisma. Haven't you learned anything since we've been working together?"

Dawes frowned, stung. He had learned much, he thought. He could translate whole phrases of Eloaech and work out, generally speaking, what sort of situations called for different sorts of speech. Yet she was still mocking him. "You won't help me."

"No," Amaia said, allowing the smile to fade away. "I won't. Maddox, you don't need me for this. You understand Ske'toa. I understand Ske'toa's language, but you've been closer to this person than anyone. You've seen the raids on the speeders, the hacking, the Hush House. Sure, you needed me for translating some of the base ideology, but that's all I've done. I may have figured out to whom the messages were being directed, but you didn't need me to figure out why. You are perfectly capable of doing this. And you don't need to worry about speaking before a large crowd. The broadcast isn't going to be on a stage, is it?"

"No," Dawes let his shoulders slump a bit, feeling some of the pressure lift at her words. "It's in the Interface centre below the Konsular offices."

"See"? Amaia smiled again and put her hand on his arm. "You'll do fine. Just talk to Ramani."

Dawes nodded. Whatever she said about not putting her studies into personal practise, Amaia certainly knew the exact right thing to say whenever Dawes needed it. But maybe that wasn't anything to do with linguistics. Maybe that was just being a good friend.

17

"Use language what you will, you
can never say anything but what you are."
—Ralph Waldo Emerson

Dawes tugged at the edge of his tunic, scowling in distaste. When Konsular Ramani had told him that he was to show up at the Interface centre at the base of the Konsular offices, Dawes had assumed that he would be in a clean room with no one else there besides the Konsular and the camera-drones. He had not thought that he would be in the actual Interface centre, where it was freezing, and all of the Interfaces were in their alcoves, wires and tubes coming out of their bodies. The lights were dim, a dark blue, making the shadows long. He hated being around Interfaces.

"Over here, Inspector," a caretaker waved his hand, gesturing Dawes to a well-lit circle in the midst of the Interfaces. The lights cast the walls into complete darkness so you couldn't see the Interfaces themselves. It was a comfort to Dawes and, he imagined, the people who would be watching the broadcast. He certainly didn't want to be discussing Ske'toa amongst all of the people wired up to the computers.

Konsular Ramani was already waiting in the circle, standing at one of the podiums set up before the camera drones bearing the Republic seal of infinity. He nodded solemnly to Dawes as the Inspector approached. "Citizen. You are here in good time."

"Why are we down here? There have to be better places for this."

Dawes hunched his shoulders and glanced towards the Interfaces. He couldn't see them, thank the Republic, but he knew they were there, and he knew that their eyes were staring blankly ahead, like corpses.

"This is one of the most secure places in all of Kyper," Ramani looked grave. "We didn't want any interference."

"You think Ske'toa would have openly attacked the broadcast?" Dawes scoffed. "Ske'toa hasn't openly attacked anything except those speeders, and those were just a series of bash-and-dashes, done in the dark hours of the morning. No witnesses. Ske'toa doesn't attack things openly."

"Be that as it may," Ramani's voice was stiff, as if he didn't like having his plans contradicted, "we wanted this broadcast as secure as possible, and the best way to achieve that is to hold it here. The security is such that people can't just walk in here, nor does anyone know where this is coming from. We're scrambling the signal so that its location can't be fixed."

Dawes shrugged, but he had his doubts. If Ske'toa wanted to do something about the broadcast, scrambling the signal would be pointless. The best hope they had was to get on the air before Ske'toa knew anything about the broadcast, and perhaps they could make it through before Ske'toa figured out how to hack them. Honestly, Dawes fully expected to be cut off at some point, but at least he knew what sorts of things he was going to say. Amaia had been right. He knew Ske'toa. He wasn't as politically suave as the Konsular, but he figured he could make a speech.

A man stepped forwards with a box of what looked like powders and pieces of metal. Dawes scowled at the man and said to Ramani, "I'm not wearing make-up."

"This is a broadcast, Inspector. For you to show well on camera, we need to highlight some of your features. Including your age. Oh, and you will wear a pin on your tunic to match the Konsulars." Ramani waved his hand dismissively as a woman approached him with a similar box.

"Highlight my age?" Dawes asked incredulously. The man replaced the silver emblem with a gold circle and infinity on Dawes' chest and started doing something to his hair.

"Age indicates that you've lived a fully dutiful life to the Republic. You are still working for the good of the Republic and in your wisdom, you are the best one to capture Ske'toa. It's all nonsense, but the public approves," Ramani said.

"It *is* nonsense. I'm a good Inspector because I was Placed as one, not because I have wisdom or a full life or whatever," Dawes scoffed. He glared again at the man with the powders and the man finally scurried away to vanish in the darkness that hid the Interfaces. Ramani said nothing to Dawes' words, just smirked and shook his head.

"You are prepared to talk about Ske'toa?" Ramani said, stepping up to a podium and adjusting it minutely.

Dawes nodded.

"Good. I will give a brief introduction and ask a question. You will then answer and expound on anything I ask. If you don't know, make it up. I don't care whether Ske'toa believes everything you're talking about tonight, only that the general populace believes it to be bad for them."

In other words, Dawes thought with a grimace, we don't care what you say, as long as the people believe it. He let out a slow breath through his nose, no longer nervous about making the speech. It was a waste of words meant to soothe people into complacency with the current regime of the Republic. Dawes believed wholeheartedly in the Republic, but he had seen the darker side of the people currently running things, and it was no wonder the Republic was stagnating. If the Konsulars were using Dreamscape, the Military Intelligence did nothing but watch, the Tech Elite utilised their time maintaining whatever technology they already had, what could one expect? The duty amongst the current lot was obviously waning.

"When is this meant to begin?" Dawes growled out, straightening his shoulders. His duty hadn't waned. He had his doubts, mostly to do with Ske'toa and whether or not he was going to find the rebel, but his sense of duty was whole. He could talk to a bunch of people. It was his duty to reassure them, no matter how much effort the Konsulars cared to put in.

"In just a few moments. You'll hear a ring and then I will start," Ramani said. The Konsular slipped his hand into his pocket and pulled out a syringe, and, just as quickly, jabbed it into his arm. Dawes recoiled in shock.

"Should you be doing that now?" he said in an undertone, though only the Interfaces and their caretakers remained to hear.

"Better now than in the middle of the broadcast," Ramani said in the same low voice. His shoulders had already relaxed, and he had taken on the calm, confident, positive look that Dawes associated with what the leaders of the Republic should be. The idea that all those images were based on drug-addicted politicians was repugnant. Before he had time to school his expression, there was a bright chime and Ramani started talking.

"Good evening, Citizens of the Republic. As you may very well know, there has recently been a series of dissident behaviours throughout the city, resulting in power outages, strange languages appearing on the Interface, even the death of one of our most respected citizens.

These incidents are said to be under the guidance of one known only as Ske'toa. Many rumours have abounded as to the reason for Ske'toa's rebellion and what the Konsulars have been doing about the matter. The reason for this special broadcast, my dear Citizens, is to explain and dispel these rumours, and assure you that this rebel, Ske'toa, is nothing more than a menace, determined to cause as much chaos as possible, before inevitable capture. I have with me the leader of the investigation against Ske'toa, Inspector Dawes of Kyper Central, who has graciously agreed to help—"

"Are you not going to introduce me?" a distorted voice sounded through the speakers around the lighted area, neither male nor female nor machine and yet perfectly, horribly clear. The calm facade Dawes had worked to build up while Ramani was talking fell away in one shudder of fear, loathing and grudging, resented admiration. This person, this speaker, needed no introduction to Dawes. "Ah, I see that the Inspector knows who I am. Would you do the honours, *Citizen*?"

"Ske'toa," Dawes spat out, unsure as to whether he was complying with the request or just cursing the name. There was a rustling from outside the lighted area. Dawes turned his head instinctively, ready to fight Ske'toa should the rebel appear.

"I am not there, Inspector. At the moment, I believe it is more prudent for me to remain hidden, at least until such time as my beliefs can be accepted without immediate attack. However, I am here to answer your questions," Ske'toa said, sounding pleased. Ramani choked out a strangled cry which may have started as words. "Is there something the matter, Konsular? You did say that you wanted to hold this broadcast in order to explain away the rumours surrounding my recent activities. I am here to explain."

Ramani looked off to one side, likely hoping to catch the eye of the caretaker, who was helping to run the broadcast. There was no response. Dawes didn't need Ske'toa's next words to know what had happened. "I think the people would rather hear what it is that I and my associates believe straight from me, without you twisting my words. I have ensured that the broadcast will continue until everything has been answered and explained. Then, I say let the people decide for themselves which system they prefer."

"Choice again," Dawes spat, hate making him stand up straighter in order to face down his enemy.

"Of course, Inspector. Choice and free will are some of the most basic of my beliefs. *Chi kai e Eloai.* A—"

"Wanderer is free," Dawes shouted, ignoring Ske'toa's following chuckle. "I know"!

"You may, but others may not. Do they understand what an Eloai, a Wanderer, truly is?"

Dawes ground his teeth but said nothing. He didn't want to explain Ske'toa's words and beliefs with the rebel there to respond. This was not what Ramani had promised him. Frankly, he wasn't certain that he could go head to head against Ske'toa and come out quite the same. Dawes glanced at Ramani, who was standing there with his lips in a straight line and a grim expression on his face. He gave Dawes a slight nod to answer. Dawes understood—not answering would give Ske'toa a leg up in the eyes of the public, but he didn't like it.

"The Eloai are a people from ancient times who would wander about and gather stories and experiences in order to…to see what it was that made a successful society. They would not interfere in the lives they watched, as free will and the ability for a person to choose were essential to them," Dawes ground out.

"Very good, Inspector. Yes, they were Wanderers, seekers of truth and knowledge, working towards a better, more successful society. Why were some groups moral and others not? Why did a people in one spot have better technology than another only a few days journey away? They decided that an individual who chose what his or her life would entail was far more successful than one who did not."

Again, Dawes said nothing. This time, though, he didn't want to provoke the rebel into a debate. He should have been asking questions, trying to paint the Republic in a better light. He was not Placed for that, no matter what Amaia could tell him about his understanding of Ske'toa. That was far closer to Konsular Ramani's Placement.

"I see neither of you are willing to ask the question that logically follows this explanation," Ske'toa said, sounding disappointed. "Then, for the people of the Republic, I shall ask. What do the Eloai have to do with the Republic?"

"You believe that the Republic doesn't allow people choice. That it stifles a person when choice is taken away," Dawes breathed. He clapped his mouth shut a moment later, horrified that the words had slipped out. It was nearly irresistible, though, to be able to enter into conversation with the person he had been studying so intensely. Terrible, frightening and very, very alluring.

"Is that such a farfetched assumption?" Ske'toa asked. "From the moment a child is born, it knows that it will be Placed, that the Republic will determine the course its life will take. There is no point in discovering hidden talents or passions because the Republic will not take any of that into account. All that matters is Placement. What choice does this child have in deciding the course of its life? Has anyone ever asked you whether you wanted to be an Inspector for Kyper Central, or whether a Medic wants to see blood and disease every day, or whether an Interface wants to be wired into a computer and give up nearly all of its conscious thought? How can society benefit from that? It's nothing more than slavery."

"No!" Ramani hissed, eyes burning. Dawes turned to look at the Konsular and they exchanged a glance of pain for the fact that Ske'toa's words held a ring of truth. "It isn't slavery"! The Konsular tightened his fingers around the edge of the podium until the knuckles turned white, quite a feat considering his caramel skin. Dawes also saw a hint of fear behind the indignant anger that coloured Ramani's expression. When the Konsular looked desperately to him, Dawes intervened, speaking almost without realising what he was saying.

"The people of the Republic are working towards a better society by utilising their talents as best they can. The Placement discovers what the child is best suited for, both genetically and through aptitude, so that each person may do their best duty for the Republic," Dawes said.

Ske'toa laughed, actually laughed, at Dawes' words. "You don't believe that, Inspector! It's in your voice. Just because the Republic hides behind the facade of duty, saying that each person is *chosen* for their role, that they were *destined* to be Placed wherever they are doesn't mean it's not slavery. There is still no choice in the matter, no appealing to passion or talents. Aptitude, do you say? I say the Placement is based on nothing more than the whim of its leaders, the Konsulars. Isn't that right, Konsular Ramani?"

"No." This time, the word was whispered and Ramani looked slightly green. "The Placement is determined based on genetics and the aptitude of the child—"

"Oh, I don't doubt that you take genetics into account," Ske'toa said, sounding of a sneer. "But more as a measurement of how your society is shaping up. Gathering the child's genetics for Placement is just another means of taking stock of your people. You keep all the measurements in the Interface, but that plays a minimal part in Placement. Yes, certainly, you wouldn't want a person predisposed towards muscle weakness to perform physical labour. Nor would you want someone who wasn't compatible with the Interface wiring to be selected for the job. But everything else is left up to where the Konsulars believe the person is needed most or where they want the person to be."

"The Placement aptitude tests are carefully administered by the Interfaces so that—"

"You Konsulars have lists on your private servers with the names of all the children up for Placement next testing session with notes as to how you would like them Placed. The Head of the Republic gives most interesting suggestions. For example: *To Konsular Tefiri, make certain that the offspring of the Head of Maintenance are Placed lower down, as Cooks or Delivery Personnel. To Konsular Mara, the child of your sister is to be Placed within CoreTech, for your devoted service to the Republic.* There are many more notations such as this. Need I continue?" Ske'toa asked, almost politely.

Dawes felt his muscles freezing into place as Ske'toa explained the process. Amaia had suggested that a person could move beyond Placement if dedication were applied, that it was more a willingness to work and make something of your life than blindly obeying Placement and orders, not moving unless told. However, having evidence of the uselessness of Placement—apart from fulfilling the manipulations of the Konsulars—was enough to make even him start to question things. The Republic was, in the last three generations, built on Placement, on making life easier for its people so as to allow society to progress. It was not meant to be built on corruption and the manoeuvrings of politicians.

"There is no need," Ramani said, his voice little more than a whisper.

Dawes spoke, this time as a need to know rather than to argue, "If you take away Placement, though, how will people know where they are best suited?"

"By exploration, just as the Eloai did. By trying different things and seeing what suits. It comes down to choice and the willingness to work," Ske'toa replied. "Things which the Republic lacks."

"There's still a problem, though," Dawes tried to hide how desperate his voice was becoming, but he simply couldn't fathom that the system he had been upholding all his life was so wrong. "Not everybody has the willingness to work."

"That is true," Ske'toa said, voice biting. These people were obviously a sore point with the rebel. "There are people who would rather have others provide for them, making life easier and doing no work as long as they can help it. Laziness gets you nowhere, not even in the Republic as you know it. Those who do not fulfil their duty are punished, am I correct? Sent to the Rabesh Colony in order to work mindlessly like prisoners, monitored and kept under precise control. This is what was to happen to the late Daleni Itar, right, Konsular?"

"How did you—"

"I chose to learn how computers work, dear Konsular, so there is very little that can be hidden from me. I would not normally breach moral etiquette so freely were there not the fates of many millions of people riding on this fact. My motives, however, are beside the point. Was Daleni Itar, former Head of Kyper Central, to be sent to Rabesh?"

Ramani licked his lips and swallowed, saying nothing. Dawes imagined the Dreamscape was well on its way out of his system; indeed, the Konsular's hand was beginning to tremble slightly.

"Yes," Dawes said, his voice clear. "She was. And, before you ask, yes, she committed suicide rather than face the shame of having failed in her duty. Howev—"

"She didn't fail in her duty, though, did she, Inspector? She was punished for *your* failure to find and capture me," Ske'toa snapped. A dry laugh. "Such a waste. Punishing those who had nothing to do with matters in order to protect yourself so that you might catch me. All for public morale."

Dawes straightened his shoulders, his earlier dismay at the shaking of his foundation gone. The anger at this rebel, this person who chose to defile everything Dawes loved, had returned. "I do not say that such an act was right," he snarled, "but under your own ideology, isn't a person meant to make mistakes in order to learn? Isn't that how one explores, tries out new things? Alright, fine, then the Konsulars obviously made a mistake."

"That is awfully forgiving of yo—"

"I'm not done," Dawes said, voice dropping. "I want to know why you think that morality and motives should be pushed aside to promote your cause. You think that it is okay to break into the private servers of the Konsulars because the situation calls for it? Under that same reasoning, murder is perfectly acceptable if I can explain that the situation calls for it. Or is ignoring morality only for you?"

"You are very direct," Ske'toa said flatly. The rebel sounded displeased, even angry, and Dawes wanted to grin a victory. Ske'toa was still out of reach, though, only a disembodied voice and still— to Dawes' mind—winning the verbal sparring match. "However, you assume that I am throwing morality aside in all circumstances. Under your premise, a person who can explain murder as being worthwhile and necessary would thrive. That is not the case. A person who works for his or her own self-interest, or in other words, exercises free will in the pursuit of a better life, will not knowingly cause harm to his neighbours. This would cause them to retaliate in kind and, ultimately, result in a downward spiral. Each person must check the other with the result that actions that benefit one will end up benefiting others in order to provide a better life. Share food for payment of shelter, that sort of thing."

"That's it? A person must be moral because it is beneficial to them to keep his neighbours happy?" Dawes scoffed. "And if a person has no desire to pay any attention to his neighbours? That person could do irreparable harm to society for lack of…"

"Empathy? Certainly, Inspector, such an instance could happen under lawless circumstances. I am not suggesting such a thing. I suggest only that the people agree upon the laws they live under, rather than submit blindly to a ruling elite who pays no mind to anyone but themselves. Free will, not slavery, working together to create a whole. Mutual agreement, working with one another rather than separately. These are the things I set forth as an alternative to the current system," Ske'toa said.

Dawes shook his head, wanting to push aside the logic he saw in those ideas. There were flaws, certainly. Obvious ones and ones that were likely to crop up later, but they were definitely there. Yet, he could not deny the fact that Ske'toa was making sense. The words were persuasive and reasonable. Dawes wasn't certain it was the right way, though.

"What would you have the people do, then?" Ramani demanded with a sneer in his voice. "Riot against all that gives them food, shelter, clothing, community and a sense of purpose?"

"They are fed, yes, but they cannot cook," Ske'toa replied cooly. "If there were only raw food instead of delivered meals, all but the cooks would starve. So, yes, your populace is fed, but they are also dependent on the feeder. They are not capable of being independent. Everything is based upon the Republic as a sometimes-benevolent master, giving food and shelter in exchange for the blood toil of their empty minds and the repetitive motions of their bodies. The people don't even interact with others outside of their commune and Placement. No Cook would be caught dead in a Factory Worker's commune, nor would a Konsular deign to talk with a mere Clerk unless it was of the greatest importance. These people are living with others who are meant to believe they are exactly alike. There's no discussion of philosophy or how something works, no exchange of ideas or beliefs. This broadcast is likely the first time any of these people have heard more than the propaganda they are spoon-fed as children. That's not freedom."

"You intend to force them to choose," Dawes realised, looking upwards to where the voice of Ske'toa was resonating the loudest. It was black beyond the lights of the ring where he and the Konsular stood. It was almost as though they existed in a separate world. It would not do to forget, though, that every person in the Republic was likely watching the broadcast.

"Forcing a choice would hardly be a real choice, now would it?" Ske'toa mocked.

"It's still a choice," Dawes copied Ske'toa's tone, twisting his features into anger. "You're feeding the people information about how you think things are run—and some of them may even be true. You're telling them that the Republic is making slaves of them and presenting a single alternative in order to force people to choose. Either they keep quiet and accept the system as it currently stands, or they fight back and accept your position. Slaves or freedom, isn't that what you're making them choose?"

"I'm not *making* them do anything," Ske'toa hissed. Dawes felt inner satisfaction. He was getting to the rebel. He was breaking down the logical and prepared exterior in favour of what lay beneath. He knew Ske'toa better than just about anyone and he was going to show that to the entire Republic. They deserved to understand just what they were looking at.

"So, they could do nothing. Now that they have the information, doing nothing is a *choice*," Dawes raised his voice, so the last word rang in the cavernous Interface centre.

Ske'toa matched his tone, "*They don't know the meaning of the word!*"

Something clicked inside Dawes' mind and he nodded, tongue suddenly numb. He knew who Ske'toa was.

"I do." The voice was weak, barely discernible amongst the pounding in Dawes' ear. It sounded as though it was a voice that hadn't been touched in years, like it was a limb just recently rediscovered. "I know the meaning," the voice said haltingly. The lights went dark and amidst the darkness, there was a wailing, as though someone had just discovered a horrible crime.

Dawes felt that wailing resonate in his bones. He knew Ske'toa. When no more words came from the rebel, Dawes knew also that Ske'toa knew him. Dawes knew there would be no more debate that night. The time for speaking was over. Now, it was time to act.

18

"As societies grow decadent, the language grows decadent, too. Words are used to disguise, not to illuminate, action: you liberate a city by destroying it. Words are to confuse, so that at election time people will solemnly vote against their own interests."
—Gore Vidal

It took a moment for the people left in the Interface centre to realise that the lights weren't coming back on.

"What's going on, Caretaker?" Ramani growled. There was a bump and a crash and a snarled curse of both dismay and fury. Dawes gathered that the Konsular had knocked over his podium in trying to escape the darkness.

"The Interfaces…they're gone," the Caretaker replied in a small voice. There was more rustling, presumably as the Caretaker checked the Interfaces. A dark fear seeped into Dawes' mind.

"What do you mean 'gone'?" he asked slowly.

"I mean they're dead. They've all…they committed suicide," the Caretaker's voice was wobbling, as though he couldn't believe something so atrocious could have happened. Ramani's mutters in the dark halted for a moment.

"Is that even possible?" the Konsular asked dreadfully.

"The Interfaces were hooked to the computers in such a way that their conscious thoughts were given over to the computer functions, leaving the subconscious whole. Some of the bodily functions like eating and sleeping fell away, which is why we had to supplement their existence, but we were keeping them calm."

Suggesting, Dawes thought bitterly, that if the Interfaces were not sedated, they would have been far from calm. He recalled the scream that followed the second blackout of Ske'toa's attacks and the way it had echoed through the city. Perhaps the sedative had been taken away from the Interfaces for a brief moment.

The Caretaker continued talking, as if an explanation were the only thing keeping him going. "It has happened before," his voice was querulous, trembling. "When the subconscious breaks through to the conscious mind long enough to issue a command."

"What command?" Ramani asked. Dawes closed his eyes, despite the oppressive darkness.

"*Stop*," the Caretaker whispered. The sound echoed through the Interface centre, leaving silence in its wake. Dawes opened his eyes and saw a faint glow being emitted from the alcoves in which the dead Interfaces rested. The lights along the sides were coming back online.

"The Interfaces are gone," Dawes said, assessing the situation. "Does that mean the computers are gone, too? I mean, the Interfaces weren't actually the computers, they were just connected to them, right?"

"Yes." Dawes could see the Caretaker, bent before one of the alcoves, wringing his hands together. The Caretaker swallowed and cast a nervous glance at the alcoves, where the bodies lay. "They are not the computers, but they did enhance the computational power of the computers. Memory was one of the main components. Processing power. Millions of neurons in millions of Interfaces…you can't imagine how weak the computer processing will be now that they're gone. Holoscreens? No. Speeder navigation? It'll have to be done manually.

Even the security grid is too much to handle. You might—and I stress *might*—be able to get basic communications and scanning going, but the device would have to be hand held and short range."

Dawes tightened his mouth into a thin line to hold back a shout of fury. He needed to get after Ske'toa. Ske'toa had murdered these people, just like Ske'toa had murdered Daleni Itar. Oh, it wasn't conventional murder. There was no physical connection. But Ske'toa had introduced those insidious ideas and the entire infrastructure of the Republic was about to collapse. He had to find that rebel and stop any further destruction. To do that, he needed resources.

"Konsular," Dawes barked at the still-prone man. Ramani looked up, his eyes wide and the pupils dilated, not from Dreamscape but from adrenaline and fear. "People in the city are going to be panicking. I need you to get a message out as quickly as possible telling everyone to stay inside."

"How in the Republic am I meant to do that?" Ramani cried.

Dawes jerked his head towards the Caretaker, "He seems capable enough with computers. Get him to rig up a communication stream, even if it is only audio."

"I wasn't Placed for that," the Caretaker protested. "I was meant to tend Interfaces"!

"In case you haven't noticed, the Interfaces are dead. Or didn't you hear? Ske'toa wants to herald in a new age and this is its beginning. I suggest you put that computer savvy to good use and go with the Konsular. People need to be calmed down or we're going to have full-scale riots on our hands."

"Who gave you the authority to—" the Caretaker started.

"I did," Dawes snarled. "Because I am obviously the only one willing to act and make the hard choices right now. Yes," he continued at the flinching of the Caretaker, "I said choice. The time for blindly following orders is over. There is no one capable of giving orders anymore except me. So go help the Konsular and get a message out to the people!"

The Caretaker squawked in dismay but ran to help Ramani. The two of them hurried to the now-visible exit and started climbing out of the Interface centre, taking stairs that hadn't been used in who knows how long. The lifts weren't working, after all. Dawes followed after them, urging them silently to move faster, running at their heels. When they reached the ground floor level of the centre, Ramani and the caretaker started moving towards the offices. Dawes turned towards the door.

"Wait!" Ramani called, "Where are you going?"

"I have a meeting," Dawes hissed through his teeth. "I'm going to find Ske'toa."

"You know who..." the Konsular couldn't seem to bring himself to say the words. There was something there, a fear that Dawes hadn't before seen in the man, that made it impossible to say the name.

"I know," Dawes said with assurance. His very bones hummed with the knowledge and he knew that if he didn't get away from the Konsular and Caretaker soon that he would lose the rebel. He started to leave again.

"Wait!" Ramani repeated, this time sounding more desperate than before. Dawes roared in quiet frustration.

"What is it?" he snapped. "What do you possibly need that is more important right now than finding and catching Ske'toa"?!

Salesh Ramani hesitated. "What am I meant to say to everyone? About why the Interfaces are gone and what's going to happen next? About...about Ske'toa?"

Dawes took the precious seconds to pinch the bridge of his nose and take in a deep breath. He needed to be out in the city, doing his level best to put an end to the reign of Ske'toa before it truly began. "I don't care," Dawes said with a malicious snarl. "I'm not the politician. You are. Tell them the truth, for all I care! Tell them that the Interfaces committed suicide at Ske'toa's words, because that was better than living in what might be excruciating pain in order to supply the luxuries we use. Tell them that the government is corrupt and that the Placements were nothing more than a way to keep the people in line. Tell them whatever you want. I don't care."

"You are going to catch Ske'toa?" Ramani asked. This question, Dawes answered with relish.

"Yes," he said, turning and striding out the door, "I am."

The speeders were down. The computer network had recovered enough to bring on the lights to Kyper, but everyone was trying to discover what happened and were doing that by messing with holoscreens and datastreams, seeking out feeds from news networks that were no longer on air; and all of the futile activity was doing nothing but overloading the now-weakened system. They would have to start functioning without, Dawes knew. Life was going to be changed dramatically. There was no way to pretend that things were ever going to be the way they were. The Interfaces were dead. People were aware of the corruption they had been living under and Ske'toa had done the unthinkable: given them the option to realise things.

Comprehending what would happen in the future and how people would live was beyond Dawes' concern. He didn't know and he couldn't spare the energy to think about such things. All he knew was that the speeders were down, and he would have to run or walk to get to where he was going. He had relied on computers for so long that he wasn't even sure whether he would be going the right direction. But he started out.

Dawes was, surprisingly enough, one of the few people that was actually out on the street. The few others he passed had a sort of stunned, vacant expression on their faces. The rest were nowhere to be seen. As he jogged through the city, Dawes did hear Ramani's voice starting over the airwaves. Radio. The caretaker had figured out how to get the Konsular onto the radio, a system built into every computer in the city but unused for years.

"...this is a very confusing time for everyone," Ramani's voice sounded sure and yet not conciliatory. He was not apologising. He was explaining. "To have the corruption within the ranks of the Konsulars pointed out is horrifying. I do not know what my fellow Konsulars were thinking or what they hoped to gain from such manipulation of you, our beloved people. All I can do is assure you that I had no knowledge of such affairs and apologise for those that did."

Lies, Dawes broke his focus long enough to think the word. He turned a corner and grinned wolfishly as he recognised the street. He was getting closer.

"I know you have questions," Ramani continued. "About what happened this evening and what the future may bring. I will try to answer as many of them as I can, but ultimately, the way we move forwards is up to you. I can tell you that this evening, as a direct result of the words of Ske'toa, the Interfaces broke through a drug-induced stupor and committed suicide. Apparently, unbeknownst to me as a Konsular, or you as the people of the Republic, the Interfaces were forced into a near-comatose state in order to access their conscious mind for the use of enhancing our computer system. The words of Ske'toa regarding the corruption of our governing body and the necessity for choice was heard by a few. They then spread the information across the entire Interface system, initiating the mass-suicide. To those whose family members had been Placed as Interfaces, I can only apologise. I had no idea that such a terrible thing was happening to those people. I, like you, thought only of the honour in serving the Republic.

"You may wonder at my opinions, believing them to be nothing more than a means with which to placate you, but that is not the case. I was there, talking with Ske'toa as you know, and I heard the words, too. I heard the undeniable truth about other Konsulars and about the near-slavery that the government has been foisting on the people. I can accept that a new means of living and searching for a better society must be tried. I don't know if all that Ske'toa preaches is true, however. To rely wholly on a single person's need to better his or her circumstances is nothing more than relying on greed in order to maintain an ethical society. We have seen what greed and lust for power has done with the other people in the governing body. And now, they are silent, unable to form a defence."

Ramani's voice faded for a moment as Dawes turned another corner. The architecture of the city changed slightly; the communes were closer together and made of stone instead of metal and glass. A block later, and the buildings began to be made of concrete. He had made a wrong turn somewhere. Dawes cried out in fury and swung his fist, desperately hoping to hit something. He stopped a moment before hitting the stone on a building, saved only by the knowledge that he would need full use of his limbs when he met with Ske'toa. He had no nanites to heal his hand. The experiments from a generation, maybe two, ago were gone. He didn't even know if they would work without the Interfaces and he wasn't going to try. Dawes turned around and chose a different direction, heading east instead of south. He passed a building with the window open on the ground level and Ramani's words floated through the air.

"… No matter that the corruption was present, and the lack of choice given to a person was true, we must consider what is best for everyone, not just a single person, as Ske'toa would have us believe. Can a society where we have been working for so long for everyone else, where we have been selflessly pursuing a goal of betterment—no matter that our superiors had been taking advantage of us—survive when we turn ourselves over to self-interest? I don't believe that. I can't believe that. Now that we are aware of our lack of choice, I say that we seek that out. I also say that we do not forget what our predecessors built: a community. We are still a single people. We are still the Republic. We are still working for the greater good. Who's to say that we can't do that and choose the direction our lives will take? Ske'toa, for one.

"Remember, dear people, that for all of the truth behind Ske'toa's words, there were crimes and wrongdoings. This started as attacks against innocent people just so that this dissident could gain the attention of those in power. Once that attention had been given, the attacks became widespread, including blackouts where no communications could get through. If there was someone injured who needed to call a Medic, that person was stranded. Those in a position to help and assuage fear could not, because Ske'toa wanted to be heard. Then there was the terrible cost of Daleni Itar. A woman who was at the height of her career and heard what Ske'toa had to say. When the corruption of those in power sought to blame her for the lack of progress on the Ske'toa case, she *chose* to cry out against the misuse of power by killing herself. The Interfaces performed the same act, screaming out in horror at the wrongs done to them and taking the only option they saw: death.

"Ske'toa's message may have been worth hearing, my people. I heard the words. I felt them in the core of my being. But I must also ask whether the means of delivering the message was worth the message sent. Was it worth the death of millions of people in order to point out the corruption in our system? I don't believe that. Should we thank Ske'toa for bringing these issues to light? Maybe. I also think we should call this person out for the crimes committed. A terrorist may still get the questions right occasionally. But at what cost? In this case, an insurmountable one.

"I am here tonight, ashamed at what my fellow Konsulars have done in the ruling of the Republic. I am also ashamed because I did not know what was happening. I did not see it, trusting in the Placement and the desire to do my duty for the Republic in order to seek out a better life for everyone. I now know that my authority as a Konsular comes from a misguided system that Placed people at the whims of others. Therefore, I can only request of you not to panic. Inspector Dawes, whom I was with when Ske'toa interrupted our press conference, is hunting the terrorist. Soon, Ske'toa will be in custody and the dissident will be held accountable for the terrible crimes committed against the Republic. To allow this to happen, though, I ask that you remain indoors. Reflect on what has happened and about what to do in the future. We can rebuild our fractured society, but this time it will be built on what people choose is best for them.

"I propose that tomorrow, once our good Inspector has captured Ske'toa and we have all had time to think about things, that each commune pick a representative to discuss what the future will hold. I will be at the Konsular offices and we can talk as long as is necessary.

We will rebuild the Republic into a better society, just as our ancestors wanted. We may have faltered for a moment in time, but we must always look to the future. And now, we will do it together. Thank you, good people, for all that you have done and will continue to do. The Republic would be in shambles but for your faith. Good night, dear Citizens."

As Ramani's voice faded into silence, Dawes found his steps leading him exactly where he needed to be. He was breathing heavily from jogging and running and pure adrenaline. He no longer felt to be a man in his seventies. He was as young and vigorous as he had ever been. This was what he was meant to be doing, Placement or not. The thrill that came with discovering who was behind the wrongs of society and bringing them down was all that he needed.

It occurred to him that the drive to hunt and catch criminals was what might have made him so unpopular with the others at Kyper Central. They might have been Placed there, but they now knew what that meant. Absolutely nothing. No, Dawes knew in that very moment that even if he had been given a choice, he would be standing exactly where he was just then. He was going to catch Ske'toa, whatever the consequences.

His steps echoed oddly against the pavement. The University had always been quiet, with people studying to become subject-experts more inclined to spend time in an Interface room or sifting through data. That night, though, it was dead. There was not a soul to be heard. Even the insect and animal life that lived in the gardens were quiet. Dawes heard only the pounding of his heart in his ears.

He walked across the campus as quickly as his old legs would manage. He had gotten his breathing under control but didn't want to run. He cursed that choice a moment later when he reached the building just off-campus. The lights, unlike the rest of the city, were dark. Dawes stepped through the door, somehow his security clearance from Kyper Central still letting him in. He waved his hand for the lights and they flickered weakly to life, another drain on the already strained system.

The office was in ruins. The books that he and that person had poured over in their quest for understanding were torn asunder. Pages were strewn on the floor and the notes that she had painstakingly written out by hand were in shredded pieces. The only thing that was whole was the board where she wrote.

Dawes let out a roar of fury that rattled the windows and echoed through the dead night. Written on the board in those same mocking tones as the note left in the Hush House was a message meant for him.

You finally asked the right question. Kair chere ta.

I congratulate you, Dawes translated silently. He bared his teeth in response and turned to the chaos in the room. He would find some scrap of information that would lead him to the person he had been convinced was the one person he could trust. After all, words meant everything.

19

Skiya looked up from where she had been tearing apart the computer components as the door opened. Skiya straightened into a semi-salute, barely managing to miss hitting her head on the overhang of the ductwork. "Ske'toa!" Skiya exclaimed in surprise.

"Hello, Skiya," Amaia said in a low voice, the remnants of a snarl on her features. "What are you doing"?

"I figured if that Konsular managed to get things working, then I could, too. I mean, I know the Interfaces are down, but there is enough residual function that I should be able to get *something* to work. The whole computer system can't have been running through the Interfaces. They just enhanced it. But I can't seem to get anything except a couple of flickers through the communications array," Skiya pouted. She leaned back on her heels and threw her wire cutters aside.

"You won't get anything to work," Amaia sat on the edge of a chair, leaning back casually, just a hint of arrogance on her features. Skiya looked up at her expectantly. "The Caretaker with the Konsular appears to have been more capable than I anticipated. He managed to claim enough processing power for that…enlightening speech."

"There's too much noise," Skiya agreed, clicking her tongue in disgust at the wires. She was silent for a moment, long enough for

Devar to walk into the room from the back area, looking grim. Amaia greeted him with a calm wave of her hand.

"They've branded you a terrorist," Devar said in a low voice. Amaia laughed lowly, shaking her head. "They're going to be searching for you."

"It was actually a very smart move on their part," Amaia mused. At the horrified looks of her followers, she smiled and nodded. "Saying that I'm a terrorist stops others from flocking to me. Agreeing with some of the 'truths' I uncovered for them, while simultaneously putting the blame for the Interfaces on me confuses people enough that they'll wait before rallying to my cause. Our cause."

"But people will hate you!" Skiya protested. "How can they listen to what you have to say if they hate you"?

"It's because they hate me that they'll listen to what I have to say. Having people join the cause while thinking and asking questions because I'm meant to be such an evil person is better than having mindless drones who follow me because I'm the one who pointed out the obvious. Konsular Ramani has given himself the authority to step into my shoes and take control of the Republic. Instead of choosing between the corrupt system under which people currently live and myself, a known terrorist, there is a third option now. Ramani has become a middle ground," Amaia waved her hand dismissively.

"Then we have failed," Devar said in a quiet voice. He looked distraught at such an option and even winced when Amaia grinned and shook her head.

"No," she said. "We haven't. Don't you see? The people are still following what we believe. They're still choosing and being made to learn and think. Just because I'm not at the front of the effort doesn't mean that we've failed. In fact, I think this suits me better. I can work in the background and quietly point people in the right direction. Of course, I'll have to see about getting the computer systems fixed before my incarceration, but that shouldn't be too—"

"Incarceration?" Devar hissed the word out.

Amaia shrugged one shoulder, not looking in the least put out by the thought. Skiya shifted uncomfortably, both afraid at the thought of her Ske'toa in prison and the calm with which Amaia faced it. "Inspector Dawes knows who I am, now. I doubt very much he will rest until I am found. Or didn't you listen to the entire broadcast?"

"We did," Skiya assured, though she didn't know why.

"So, you know that he is currently wandering the city, hunting me," Amaia said.

"You're awfully calm about the matter," Devar said slowly, as if tasting the words before saying them. He watched Amaia warily, Skiya noted, though their leader chose to ignore the fact.

"How many people would listen to a word I have to say if I am wandering free amongst the people, able to strike and attack at any possible moment? It is far simpler if people believe that I am safely locked up and out of the way. I can still be heard, but of course the prison system is "infallible," and I would be no danger to anyone." Amaia shook her head, an ironic smile not quite meeting her eyes. Skiya wondered just how dangerous Amaia would have to be to find prison useful rather than life-ending.

"You can escape the Inspector," Devar was close to pleading—Skiya knew that tone—and he had stuffed his hands into his tunic pockets to keep from using them to express himself. "He can't know you're here. And the city is big enough that it wouldn't be hard to get you out. Go to Sažhem or Crepuscule. Continue your work there."

"I'm flattered that you think so much of me." Amaia fixed her eyes on Devar and graced him with a benevolent, almost indulgent smile. With a surge of emotion, Skiya realised she wanted that same recognition. As a leader to a devoted acolyte, a teacher to pupil, a friend accepting concern. She nearly thrust her hands into her own pockets to keep from throwing herself at Ske'toa's knees. "But you needn't go to the trouble. The Inspector will discover me soon enough."

"You can't know that," Skiya cried.

"I can," Amaia said firmly. "I placed the information myself, scattering it amongst my handwritten notes on Eloaech. I did not spend so much time training the Inspector in a linguist's way of analysis for nothing. He'll soon discover the warehouse where we manufacture Dreamscape. There will be a raid, but no loss of life. Though I do regret having to destroy such a useful manufacturing facility, necessary as it is—and I will be arrested. Such a public terrorist, there is certain to be an announcement of my arrest, just as there is certain to be a trial."

"They'll order you dead," Devar said.

"Will they?" Amaia asked, flicking her gaze to Skiya. Just like that, the chance for praise was offered and Skiya took it gladly.

"They wouldn't dare," Skiya said, a gleeful grin spreading over her dark features. "You showed them the corruption in the system and explained that they were living in slavery. You were responsible for the new age. They can't just ignore that."

Amaia inclined her head, "Precisely."

Devar scowled, not appearing comforted by that thought. "You trust this Inspector to just arrest you, not kill you? Isn't he fighting for everything we want…to be destroyed?"

"You use such absolute terms, Devar," Amaia smiled at her follower. Skiya wasn't certain whether she saw affection or amusement in that smile. "Destroyed? Only if absolutely necessary. I much prefer things to be changed. For the better, naturally."

Devar shifted his weight, looking like a chided child. Amaia kept her smile for a moment more before letting it fade slowly, naturally. She fingered the collar of her tunic and let her eyes glaze over. Skiya and Devar leaned closer, instinctively needing to be nearer to their leader in her time of trial. "As for the Inspector, I am certain he will want me dead. Before you protest, remember that I have not been idle these past weeks. While you have been spreading the word about our cause and sowing doubt amongst the people, I have been working with the Inspector on the same matter."

"You've been teaching him Eloaech," Skiya said, trying to hide the question in her voice. She didn't want Ske'toa to think that she didn't understand, even though it was truth.

"Amongst other things. I've been teaching him to think like other people. I've been teaching him to question the use of language as a means to understand how people—both individuals and groups—express their world. Language is the tool we use to express our world and it is also the means by which we are constrained. Teach a man a dead language of freedom and choice and working for one's own curiosity and pleasure and his own thoughts begin to change. I took the Inspector's world and twisted it, made him question his role in the Republic before he even knew that the Placement was false and that the structure wasn't sound. He started to question his capabilities and motives the moment we discussed what Eloai were. He learned to think how Ske'toa thinks and I learned how he thinks. So, yes, I know full well that he sees what I am as a betrayal, pure and simple. I also know that he will not do anything to harm me. He cares for me too much because I showed him another way, one that suited him better."

Amaia rose from her chair and started towards the window, staring out into the dimly-lit city. There was a flush in her skin that lent her a feverish look. Skiya glanced up at Devar, who returned the look with stony silence. There was something, both Skiya and Devar knew, that made this Inspector so interesting to Amaia. There was more than just the fact that she was using him to get into prison. It was more than just him being the means to get her message across to the Konsulars and the people. It was more, still, than him being the method by which Amaia kept an ear out for what the Republic knew. Skiya doubted that Ske'toa cared for the Inspector any more than she cared for the corrupt Konsulars, but surely, she wouldn't seem so excited by a confrontation otherwise. Maybe it was just the fact that this stage of the movement was coming to an end. Once she was in prison—Skiya shuddered at the thought—then the movement to change the Republic would have to take on a different, more subtle form.

"The game is coming to a head," Amaia murmured.

"You think this is a game?" Devar sounded pained. Ske'toa turned at the tone in his voice and even Skiya was surprised to see anguish in the former Medic's face. "You're our *leader*. What are we meant to do when you're gone?"

"I'm not going to die, Devar, and even if I did, you think that I wouldn't have prepared for that contingency?" Amaia shook her head. "Your concern is appreciated, but unnecessary."

"But—" Devar started, looking for all the world like a child about to lose its parent.

"Enough," Ske'toa interrupted. All the affection and smiles and pride that had previously been on her face was gone, leaving only hardness and a carefully concealed fury. "I know what I am doing. Your…efforts for the cause are noted and appreciated, but I go on alone from here. I started this and I intend to finish it. Am I understood?"

There was no need for her to repeat herself. Ske'toa, the mover of worlds, had spoken. Devar and Skiya nodded, saying nothing. Skiya felt as though her tongue had been plastered to the roof of her mouth and a shiver went down her spine. This, she thought, was the reason why Ske'toa had been so feared. Not because she could infiltrate the computers or reveal corruption in a government, but because she was fixated on her goal at the peril of all who stood in her way. There was no fond farewell between this person and her devoted followers, only a brief nod and the whisper of the door as it opened and closed behind her.

Devar was the first to break the silence that had fallen on the room. He shuffled around to sit in the chair recently vacated by Amaia and stared at the door. "She's going to be killed," he said.

"And what would you have us do? You heard her. She knows what she's doing. If she thinks that the Inspector won't kill her, then she's right. He'll have caught his terrorist. She can still work when she's in prison and—"

"And you don't believe that any more than I do," Devar snapped. Skiya folded her arms, glaring.

"Oh"?

"You know full well that Ske'toa will do whatever is necessary for the cause. It's her entire life, taking down the system of slavery and brining about choice. No more grovelling to a heartless master. Instead, choosing what you do with your life and working to make it happen. Ske'toa would lead us to that future," Devar spoke reverently, a slight smile touching his mouth.

"You think she is that power hungry? That she only wants a chance to lead the Republic?" Skiya snorted and shook her head.

"Who else would guide us through the confusion that follows this *coup*"?

"That fool Salesh Ramani has already claimed the throne," Skiya bit out sarcastically.

"Do you believe that he would allow Ske'toa, who has more right to that title than he, to live?" Devar snapped.

Skiya bit her lip, considering. Maybe Devar had a point. So what if Inspector Dawes didn't want to kill Ske'toa? Ramani would happily do away with her just to solidify his claim to power. He didn't need to have the person who had pointed out all the problems and offered a solution around to ruin his new reign. He needed a scapegoat for all of the problems that were about to rise up due to the loss of the Interfaces, the lack of governing body, everything. Hadn't he already branded Ske'toa a terrorist?

"What do we do?" Skiya asked softly.

"We go after her," Devar replied just as softly.

"We don't even know where she is."

"She said that the Dreamscape factory would be raided. So that's where we start." Devar rose from the chair and went to a cabinet in the far corner. He pulled out a Fyre pistol, and not one like the local Security Forces toted. This was one that blatantly broke the gun laws of the Republic. This was meant to kill.

Skiya nodded and watched as the man Placed and trained to save lives strapped that weapon to his waist. Then, in equal silence as their great leader, they walked out the door with only a whisper to announce their presence.

20

"Every word is a prejudice."
—Nietzsche

Dawes had never stepped foot in the warehouse before, yet, he knew, almost instinctively, that it was a place Ske'toa had frequented. There was something about the way it had been quietly referenced in her notes that made him certain she would be there. Whether she would be waiting for him or preparing to flee, he didn't even consider.

He stepped through the side door, grateful that the manual door didn't squeak. As soon as he stepped inside, he knew only complete darkness. The lights of the city outside didn't penetrate the skylights. Dawes froze, straining his ears to hear any sign of her. He heard nothing. His eyes adjusted enough to note that the warehouse wasn't completely dark; there was a faint line of light spilling into the large room from a door not a hundred feet from where he stood. Dawes crept towards the door, wondering for the first time in this mad hunt whether he should have put on armour. Who knew what a terrorist would do?

He slid his hand around the handle and turned it, waiting for a creak or sign that he was noticed. He had the door most of the way open and was about to slip inside when he heard, "Come in, Maddox. There's no need to wait outside."

Her voice, he knew, was exactly the same and yet it held a different note for him. He couldn't place it, only knew that it was different.

Maybe because he knew what she was now. The absence of the formal greeting rang stark in the silence, though she had rarely used it before. Everything was different, now, only for the application of knowledge.

Without saying a word, he stepped inside and drew his crowd-control weapon, a bully stick with an electrical current running through it. Ske'toa was sitting at a long table with few chairs around it. There were unpacked boxes and a collection of vials wrapped in packaging. Dawes curled his lip in disgust. Dreamscape. This was where the city drug dealers got their Dreamscape.

"I should have known you were nothing more than a common criminal," Dawes snarled, moving around the table so he was looking her straight in the eye. "Drunk on the power that controlling the drug trade gives you. Was that what made you think you could take down the Republic, Ske'toa?" Dawes spat the last word.

"Ah, yes, the name you gave me," Amaia raised her eyebrows and rolled a vial through her fingers disinterestedly. "Ske'toa, meaning malevolent spirit. You thought to show people that I was evil, doing this purely for spite. Yet look what it turned into. Now even followers of the cause use it as a symbol of hope, the creature that tore down corruption and revealed slavery. Just another example of how language evolves, is it not?"

"Don't talk to me about language," Dawes snarled viciously, slamming his bully stick onto the table. A current ran through the metal and some of the vials on the table jumped and cracked. Ske'toa lifted her hands in the instant before his weapon struck, her eyes remaining as cool as before.

"Why not? I am a linguist, Maddox. Language is what I do." She rested her hands back on the table as Dawes withdrew the stick.

"Liar," he hissed. "You only wanted to get close to the investigation.

You *used* me."

"You took everything I said at face value," she replied. "The trick to spotting a liar is to ask the right questions and read the intent of what is said, not merely the words. So, perhaps, Maddox, you should be asking why you—"

"Don't call me that!" Dawes snapped. Ske'toa looked at him in mild surprise, then her eyebrows puckered and her mouth curled into a smile that did not reach her eyes. Dawes' very mind was rebelling against the lessons she had taught him about kinesics that told him there was sadness in her gaze.

"I see," she said softly. "Very well. And to answer your accusation, *Inspector*, I am a linguist. The only qualified one in the Republic. Naturally, then, language would be my means of getting the message across. If it happened to be the means of getting involved in the investigation, then that was only a useful side effect."

"Liar," Dawes repeated, barely keeping his anger contained. His hands shook and he nearly dropped the weapon he held.

Ske'toa snarled in anger herself, throwing a vial of Dreamscape at the wall so it shattered. "I am not a liar," she declared. "I told you every inch of truth there was. You were the one who couldn't bring yourself to see what was right in front of you until tonight. Oh, yes, Inspector, I know exactly how you figured out who I am. You finally asked the right question. You asked how Ske'toa, the rebel, would have known about words and Eloaech if the records weren't in the computers and were impossibly hard to find. Not why. Not what. How. Not emotion, not feeling. Logic."

"I should kill you instead of arresting you," Dawes said, turning the words over in his mouth as he said them.

"Then kill me," Ske'toa stood, holding her arms out in open

surrender. "You won't, though. Don't deny it, Inspector. You know full well that you won't. Because even before I explained things tonight, you knew that the Republic was wrong. You knew that the Placement system counted for nothing but a way to keep track of the genetics of the people. We discussed it. Tore it to pieces. The language that Ske'toa used—that I used—told you another way to view the world. And you knew it was right!"

Dawes looked away to where the shattered glass of the vial lay, his mouth pressed together to keep from spitting out words. Words were her tender, so he would give her none. Yet she was right. He had been dissatisfied with the Republic. The time he spent in her office, trying to understand how a rebel thought and realising that the rebel made sense, it was a glorious release from his life. Before meeting Ske'toa— no, Amaia—he had been a frustrated old man, looking forward to his Decommissioning and the relative freedom that would have afforded him. He wouldn't have to worry about Placement telling him where he could and could not go and what he could and could not do. A Decommissioned man or woman was allowed to enjoy the full thanks of the Republic for the duty given. That was all that had been left for him. Then he met her.

Pure chance that he had been assigned to this investigation. Yet she had become something to him, even as she turned him into something else. She was someone who told him that thinking and working merely for the sake of discovering and passion could be worth so much more than blind obedience. She had given him a new lexicon in order to broaden his understanding of the world and he had embraced the new language with fervour.

For all of that, though, she had lied to him. That was a betrayal deeper than anything he had felt before. "The ends that you sought,"

Dawes licked his dry lips and returned his gaze to Ske'toa—no longer Amaia—still standing with her arms outstretched, "they could never justify the means. Millions dead. The Republic in shambles. People who have no other way to fend for themselves. Thousands more are going to die, from hunger when the Cooks stop feeding them, or in riots for new housing or positions, before your new world can be established. You had to know this."

"Their sacrifices will not have been in vain," she said simply, still holding out her hands.

Dawes let out a low, dry, humourless laugh. "Sacrifices, Ske'toa, implies *blind obedience.*"

She recoiled as if he had struck her. "I am nothing like those corrupt people that permitted slavery to flourish."

"It appears that you are," Dawes said. He pushed himself away from the table and walked towards Ske'toa, feeling as though the wrath and hatred that twisted her features were the first real emotions he had seen from her. "Amaia Wainright, known to the Republic as Ske'toa, I hereby place you under arrest for crimes against the Republic, including the inducement of the suicides of the Interfaces, the manufacture and sale of illegal substances, destruction of government property and… instigating a coup."

He reached for her arms to bind them. She was inches away from his grasp when the door burst open once more and two other people flew in. Dawes had never seen the dark-skinned girl or the distraught man before, but they obviously knew him, and his quarry. "No!" the man shouted and ran towards Dawes, aiming for a fight.

"Fools!" Ske'toa cried, twisting away from the girl, that same fury on her face.

The man pulled out a weapon and pointed it at Dawes. He felt his heartbeat slow and time seemed to inch by. He recognised the pistol as one similar to a collection Kyper Central had confiscated from moon colony traders months before: illegal and deadly. He took the bully stick in his hand and thrust it forwards, hitting the gun in the man's hand. It was a mistake, Dawes wanted to cry out an instant later, but it was too late. The electricity running through the stick came into contact with the metal and charged it, igniting the firing element.

There was an explosion, a roar of fire and a flash of light that knocked Dawes backwards into the table where the vials lay. He felt pain on his face and hands and also in his back where the shattered glass dug into his skin. There was a ringing in his ears that quickly turned to pleasantly tolling bells. Bliss flooded through his body and he had enough time to register the effects of Dreamscape before he slipped into unconsciousness.

21

Had he been a violent man, Ramani supposed he would have taken pleasure in the wounds he saw on Ske'toa's back as she was stitched up by the Medics. Broad cuts lacerated her back from where the explosion at the Dreamscape factory had thrown her into metal shelving. Smaller cuts on her arms and face indicated where vials of Dreamscape had exploded into her. Ramani took no pleasure in her injuries, though he did feel a twinge of regret that she had felt no pain.

He watched from behind thick glass as the Medics put her back together, their hands expertly trained. Ramani hadn't even asked whether they would want to do something different with their lives now that the Placement system had been abolished. Frankly, he had been too relieved to find people still at the hospital when the tactical team brought the bleeding Ske'toa, Inspector Dawes, and a girl he didn't recognise to the emergency ward. Dawes would always suffer terrible burn scars on his face as he had been the closest to the explosion. The girl was relatively unharmed: she suffered no more than a concussed brain and a few cuts and bruises. Ske'toa, too, would bear scars, but hers were far less damaging and would, if anyone knew about them, lend her a martyred look. Of the person holding the weapon that had exploded, the tactical team found only pieces. No one could identify the person, and Ramani supposed that Ske'toa and the girl were, perhaps, the only people who would mourn the deceased.

He certainly wouldn't.

The surgery had been progressing for some time. Long enough for Ramani to have informed the former Interface Caretaker that there would be another address to the people later that morning and to have returned to his home to bathe, dress, dose himself with his swiftly-dwindling Dreamscape supply and turn to face the day.

"If you're ready, Konsular," the Caretaker said in Ramani's ear. Ramani took a deep breath as he watched the Medics work on Ske'toa and wondered why he wasn't monitoring Dawes' progress. Fascination, he decided. This "nobody" woman, seeming average in every way but her mind, had slipped by his security forces, his Military Intelligence, had even gained the Inspector's trust to be involved in every step of the investigation. She was a nobody that was the only person who could have possibly been Ske'toa. Yet no one had seen it.

"How do you think she managed it?" Ramani asked absently. The Caretaker stepped up to the window and examined the scene before them quietly for a moment.

"I think she just knew what to say," the Caretaker replied.

Ramani nodded with a faint smile, as if to say, *Of course.*

"Good morning, dear people of the Republic," Ramani said, sitting once more in his chair and speaking to the computer terminal so that the world might hear his voice. "I hope that you had a restful night, but fear that with such momentous changes upon us all that you didn't. For that, I can only apologise. I know how difficult this must be for you. I, myself, spent the night wondering how such terrible things could have been slipped into my life without my knowledge. The conclusion I draw is that it was because we had faith in what our ancestors built and in our fellow people to do what was right and good for the Republic. I was mistaken and should have been working towards the betterment of society myself, asking questions and demanding answers. Never again will I be so complacent."

Ramani paused a moment to look around his office. He had to let the people digest what he was saying without forcing too much down their throats. A trained Konsular, he knew the value of silence. Ske'toa knew that, too. Perhaps she knew it better than he did.

"Early this morning, Inspector Dawes managed to find and capture the terrorist Ske'toa. There was a violent exchange and the result of which is that Ske'toa brought about another death—this time of an innocent citizen," Ramani kept his voice even and sad. He didn't believe his own words, but the public need never know that. Innocent? Hardly. Ske'toa's fault? Not from what the tactical team said. It was useful, though, to have another crime to pin to the crime lord's name. Crime lord, yes, Ramani decided. It was more useful than rebel and less frightening than terrorist. "Inspector Dawes is injured but will make a full recovery. The crime lord, Ske'toa, will be tried appropriately and sentenced to fulfil the punishment for such terrible acts against the Republic.

"Once more, I extend the invitation to come and meet with me today. We will open a discussion about how things should proceed. Should you want me to step down, I will do so with an open heart. Should you want to change careers or living spaces, or even just organise food stores, we will do all we can. We do this for the good of the Republic. That is all that matters."

Ramani signalled the Caretaker to end transmission with a wave of his hand. There was a slight pop from the speakers in the room as the computer handled the task. It would take a great deal of adapting to get used to the lack of Interfaces. Ramani decided that he would have to draw up an appropriation schedule for computer processing usage. Maybe some of the people in the Tech Elite would stay on and modify the system.

He reached into his pocket and pulled out a vial of Dreamscape. It was half-empty and his second to last. He knew that he should wait to take the drug until he desperately needed it. He also knew that he was about to step down into the meeting room on the ground floor and be faced with a horde of the people he had been loathsome to interact with on a daily basis. Ramani slipped the syringe into the vial and took out the dose. He ignored the Caretaker completely as he pushed the needle into his arm and depressed the plunger.

"Come," Ramani said, his voice full of authority despite the pleasure beginning to flow through his veins. "We have a world to reorganise."

If there was one thing he could say for this business with Ske'toa, it was that she had certainly cleared the way for him. This new Republic would be a good thing. All he needed to do was act remorseful and humble and the people would fall into his lap like sheep. Ramani smiled.

"Ah, Salesh," Ske'toa straightened slightly and turned her head towards the door where Ramani stood. He watched her for a moment, enjoying the hint of relief that came when he noted the bars between she and him, the way her not-quite-recovered person stretched out on the bed. In her new orange tunic and trousers, she looked less nondescript. The clothes, more than the cunning smile, made her seem dangerous. Ramani knew better.

"Ske'toa," he acknowledged.

"Congratulations are in order, I hear." She pushed herself into more of a sitting position, her slowness of movement the only sign that she was still injured. "The people decided to make you Head of the Republic. A daring feat for one such as yourself."

"You were the one who said opportunity was there if we were willing to work for it," Ramani bit back his own savage grin. He couldn't show pride to her, not yet. He needed her.

"You are obviously willing to work for it," Ske'toa nodded. She gestured to the cell and its scanty trappings. "You put the crime lord in prison. I quite like the description, crime lord. It suggests so much more than terrorist or rebel. A terrorist is working towards a cause—possibly a terrible one, but strong enough to demand death. A rebel is fighting for freedom against the oppression of a malignant order. A crime lord, though, is out for nothing more than personal gain, no matter the cost. Perhaps I should have been teaching you about linguistics rather than Inspector Dawes. You're obviously a capable student."

Ramani tightened his lips and took a deep breath, silently reminding himself that she was in prison and that he wasn't. She was in no position to bargain. He needed her and she would give him what he wanted. He *wanted* Dreamscape, but as his supply had run out nearly a week ago and the usual means of getting the drug were gone, he would have to live without. The withdrawal symptoms had nearly killed him. His body still craved it. Reality just seemed so drab without it. Considering all of his new responsibilities, drab was something he couldn't stand.

No, Ramani closed his eyes and forced down the desire. That wasn't why he was here. "We both know what you are," he said at last, surprised at the hoarseness in his voice. He opened his eyes and found

Ske'toa grinning at him. "You're what the people want."

"I am," she agreed. "But they don't know that, and you aren't going to tell them. Are you?"

"No," he admitted. "I can make things easier for you in here. Better food, better furnishings, books from outside, whatever you need."

"I can get all of that myself," Ske'toa said with a casual smile. "I know enough about people and whispering words in the right ears to make my life much easier."

Ramani remembered the words whispered in his own ear, what seemed like a lifetime ago. A suggestion and a terrible choice. He didn't doubt Ske'toa could do just as she was suggesting. That meant he had nothing to offer but her freedom, which was impossible. His mouth went dry and he felt his heart pounding in his ears. He needed, desperately, a dose of Dreamscape. Anything was better than this.

"You needn't look so distressed, Salesh," Ske'toa said with a smile. "I can get whatever I need for myself. But I will help you."

"You will"?

"Yes," she nodded. "You will owe me a favour. That is all."

He couldn't possibly imagine what favour she might want, but he didn't care. He was going to get the help he needed. The people dying and clamouring for his help would be memories of a distant past. Ske'toa would give him the tools to simply make them go away. "Done," Ramani said, the flush of success coming to his face.

"Good. I can get you *everything* you need. So why don't you begin by telling me what your current troubles are." Ske'toa leaned forwards on her bed, eyes penetrating. Ramani licked his lips and swallowed, necessity driving away fear.

The new Head of the Republic walked into his office hours later, feeling drained and humiliated. Ske'toa had given him everything he needed to solve his current problems, but behind her intelligent words and successes, there had been a mocking laughter and the knowledge that no matter what he would say, she was the one setting policy now. It became very clear that for all his rhetoric, Ramani understood little about what needed to be done to bring about the new world. By the end of the meeting with Ske'toa, he felt as though he were the one behind the bars and she ruling the Republic.

Disgusted with himself, Ramani threw his jacket across the office and stalked over to his desk to sit and hopefully bury his head in his hands. He lay his head across the desk, feeling the coolness of the finished wood, a relief. Ske'toa didn't have such luxury as a real wood desk, he thought pettily, running his fingers along the grain. And just because he consulted her opinion didn't mean that he wasn't the one running the Republic. She was behind bars, sentenced to life imprisonment for her crimes. The people wanted her to suffer for what she had done, but not to die. Some part of them, like him, understood perfectly well what it was that Ske'toa had brought about.

He just understood that better than most.

There was a knock on the door that nearly had Ramani shouting. He did not want to be disturbed right then. Without the Dreamscape, regulating his emotions was so much more difficult. He had mood swings and found himself shouting at people for being perfectly reasonable. He wanted at least another hour to himself to bring his mind back under his control and to enjoy the luxuries that were placed at his disposal by the people.

Ramani was about to call out for whoever it was to leave him alone, but the door opened before he got a chance. Ah, well, the old Caretaker.

Now his appointed technical advisor. The creature had proven shrewd and capable with the computers, even without the Interface. He didn't know everything there was to know about the systems, but what he didn't know he soon found out. Given time, the man could even prove to be as capable as Ske'toa. That thought shut down any good mood Ramani had and he leaned back in his chair, folding his arms in disgust.

"What do you want?" he bit out.

"A delivery came for you," the advisor growled in almost exactly the same tone. Capable as both of them were, that didn't stop them from quickly growing to despise one another. The taste of power was too addictive to give up, however, so they kept their mouths shut in public. "There was no courier, no stamp of address, just a box on my desk for you."

Ramani took the box and the advisor turned and stalked out of the office as quickly as he had come. Without sparing the man a second thought, Ramani tore open the box. Inside, he found a folded sheet of paper—how archaic—and a collection of vials. His muscles turned to water and he stared in absolute shock. Trembling slightly, he opened the note.

For the Head of State,
We wouldn't want you to be uncomfortable dealing with the rabble, now would we?

There was no signature, and Ramani didn't recognise the handwriting. Not that he would, given he hadn't seen handwriting since a visit to the museum years ago. There was no doubt about who it was from or the mocking tone that dripped from the words. He didn't care. Ramani just ran his fingers lightly over the top of the vials and licked his lips eagerly.

22

"You taught me language; and my profit on 't
Is, I know how to curse: the red plague rid you
For learning me your language!"
—Shakespeare, *A Winter's Tale*

This whole thing had been a mess, Dawes decided. He was standing at the window of his flat and stared out at the city. Speeder function was still questionable, so the skies were strangely clear. He had also been forced to take the stairs from the ground floor, as his speeder was not in the bay and he wouldn't have wanted to fly it in any case. His arm was still in a sling, and his left eye wasn't seeing as well as it used to. Not to mention his entire face throbbed every time he took a breath. Burns, according to the Medic who had patched him up, seemed to take more painkillers than other injuries and they just didn't have the resources. There had been an outpouring of Dreamscape into the hospital pharmacy, though. No one had known where it came from and Dawes barely dared to think his suspicions, let alone say them out loud. He had refused the drug offered to him, stating plainly that he would rather deal with the pain.

Three days later and he was still feeling as though the situation was unresolved. Ske'toa was in prison. Good riddance. The girl who had come into the warehouse with the other man was also in prison, her association with Ske'toa enough to earn a life sentence. The man, Dawes knew full well, was dead.

Ramani had been named Head of the Republic. The announcement had Dawes throwing whatever breakable items he could find in his flat. Debris was strewn everywhere. He hadn't bothered to clean it up.

That day, though, was worse than everything else. He had woken from a nightmare of fire and betrayal to the realisation that he was meant to be Decommissioned that day. Ske'toa had been his last case. It was meant to be a simple bash-and-dash with which to impress the public and put a decent stamp on his career. Instead, it had destroyed everything he had known to be true, not to mention the structure of the Republic.

Dawes considered the throbbing pain in his face and wondered if this was what Daleni Itar had felt like before she threw herself off the balcony. If so, he understood.

"Delivery," a voice called out. Dawes turned and saw a young girl wearing a courier's uniform holding a note in her hand. The youth of the Republic had stepped up during the crisis, taking jobs their elders no longer wanted in order to make ends meet. This was not the first child Dawes had seen working before their time. He stalked over to the door, the debris crunching under his foot. With a growl, he snatched the note out of her hand. She turned and fled.

Dawes took the note back to the window before he opened it, all the while considering what he was meant to do now. It took him a moment before he realised he had opened the paper and not read it. It didn't even occur to him to think a paper note odd. Until he started reading, that is.

> *Maddox Dawes,*
> *I know you wanted me to use your title, not your name, but as you have been promoted, it is now appropriate to use your entire*

name, as was done with Daleni Itar. I offer my congratulations at the promotion. Head of Kyper Central, which, as you surely know, now controls what was Military Intelligence and the local Security forces.

You once said that you wanted nothing more for this case to be over so you could attain your Decommissioning. You also said that you wanted nothing more than the chance to work and prove yourself because you were capable, not because you were Placed. I am most curious to see which of these will prove to be the truth.

Good luck at your new job. Don't forget, you captured me, so you deserve it. And, after all, the Republic needs you.

He didn't read the signature. Couldn't bear to look at the name that she used, whether it was the one he knew her by or the one he gave her. He didn't want to know which person she had become because he doubted he would like the answer.

Dawes supposed he shouldn't have been surprised that she knew about the promotion. He had only heard about an hour ago and it hadn't even been announced over the radio. Curious, he thought with a snarl. She was curious to see what he would do and which of his statements had been truth.

Dawes tore the note into tiny pieces and flung the scraps of paper out the open window. He wouldn't tell her which was truth. He would never see her again. His thoughts might turn to her every minute, but he would at least have the satisfaction of denying a face-to-face conversation. Dawes closed his eyes and counted time by the beats of his heart that sent screams of agony through his face.

He wouldn't tell her the truth, just as she hadn't told him the truth. The difference, though, was that he didn't know what was true anymore.

ACKNOWLEDGEMENTS

For as many ideas as run around my brain, writing and putting together a book is a surprisingly difficult process. I am so thankful to have so many amazing people around me to support me and listen to all my ideas and woes when I start rambling on about writing.

I would especially like to thank my dad who read the early drafts of *Speaker of Words* and told me they weren't terrible. He listened to me rant on and on about the various social issues in the Republic and didn't bat an eye when I refused to tell him who Ske'toa was. (Though, I'm pretty sure he figured it out.) He has helped me collect quotes—with some very strange sessions listening to the Eurythmics and The Clash that were more entertaining than helpful—and figure out just what needs doing in regard to getting this book ready for publication. Mostly, though, I would like to thank him for never giving up on my dream of being a writer and never telling me to go pursue something else.

I would also like to thank my editor, Vanessa at Night Owl Freelance, who has been amazing in going through *Speaker of Words* and suggesting changes to make it the best book it can be. She has helped me when I was too close to see the problems. Her edits were absolutely perfect and just what the story needed. I especially want to thank her for helping me to self-publish this book properly, rather than my previous methods of just hoping for the best. I appreciate every minute of her hard work!

Many thanks also to the Online Writing Communities. They have been the most supportive group of people when it comes to the writing and publishing processes. They are the first people I will ask for help, the ones who are willing to offer their time to make someone's work stand out, and who also write the most amazing pieces. They are the friends I never knew I had.

I could never have published this book without all of your support. If you have read this book, thank you. If you have listened to me rambling, thank you. If you have seen a post on social media and thought, "Gee, how weird!" I thank you. I could not have done any of this without all of you.

Sincerely,
E.G. Stone

Learn More and Follow Her Work at
EGStone.com

https://facebook.com/egswriter

https://instagram.com/egswriter

https://twitter.com/EGStone3

E.G. Stone is an independent author who has been writing, quite literally, since the age of six. Since then, E.G. has improved rather a lot and has written (so far) 22 full-length novels, various short stories, a screenplay, snippets of poetry, and various blog entries that may or may not make sense. E.G. enjoys writing in many different genres. Her favourites are science fiction, mystery (preferably of the murder variety), adventure, and fantasy—basically anything where the world isn't quite what you would expect. When not writing, she is off musing about the workings of languages, both real and created, or wandering around experiencing new people, places, and things. E.G. prefers to write while sitting with a cup of tea and a cat, but almost any location will do nicely. (Excepting airplanes. Or cars. Or moving vehicles at all.) E.G. has officially started pursuing this independent-author, writing-full-time thing as a career and is enjoying every minute of it—no matter how bizarre, unexpected, or just plain weird.